A NECESSARY EVIL

Electronic and soft cover print versions
Published by Jump N Jupiter

ISBN 0-9719362-8-5

Printed in the United States of America

A NECESSARY EVIL

BY

Robert Stricklin

DEDICATION

To my wife Martine,
without whom little would be possible

ACKNOWLEDGEMENT

I would like to thank Bea and Diane Jacques
for their indispensable assistance in
putting together this manuscript.

I

Okay, don't panic. You're a big girl. You can handle this.

Or so Karen thought as she cautiously watched the hooded man in the blue parka abruptly cross the street as if to meet her. His hands were stuffed in his pockets, his shoulders slouched, but there was definitely a sense of menace and purpose in his long strides and mouth-gaping intensity. The closer he approached, the more she recognized that vacant look in his hollow eyes. It was the dull, ruthless stare of a hardcore junkie. No doubt about it.

This is what I get for working late. I've got no time for any nonsense. Who needs this now?

But rather than hastening her steps to evade her apparent pursuer, Karen came to an abrupt stop, pretending not to be intimidated, forcing a confrontation. He paused several feet before her, returning her defiant glare but saying nothing, his unshaven pockmarked face barely visible in the night light of a nearby lamppost.

Well? Isn't this where you ask me if I can spare any change, and I tell you to get lost? Let's get this over with so we can get on with our lives.

But the would-be panhandler wasn't asking.

"Give me your money," he bluntly demanded.

Karen's blank stare became quizzical. They were standing on a sidewalk of a dimly lit, quiet residential street on the Upper East Side of Manhattan. It was approximately 9:15 p.m. and although the block was virtually deserted, cars and taxis were driving by and, at any moment, someone could be leaving an apartment. Was this guy for real, thinking he could frighten her into surrendering her hard-earned cash?

"Come on," he ordered, nervously looking behind him and over Karen's shoulder.

But before she could say, "I don't think so," Karen's assailant struck her across the face with the back of his hand and shouted, "Come on!"

Stunned by the blow, she backed away toward the nearest doorway.

"N-no," she barely responded, to which he angrily grabbed her by the hair and started dragging her to the nearest alleyway. She let out a braying yelp, but it was a rather feeble cry for help. She resisted as well, tugging and tussling, but he was startlingly strong and determined. Before she knew it, she was out of plain sight, secluded in a dark and dangerous place, thrown against a cold brick wall.

Whoa! Wait a minute! Wait a minute! This can't be happening. Not to me.

"Give me the money, God damn it!" he spat, trying to wrest the handbag from Karen's shoulder.

Foolishly, she flailed, trying to fend him off. She had no intention of being a victim, or making it easy for him. But then came a sharp, slashing pain. It was so swift and intense that Karen gasped and reflexively reached for her throat. As she clutched her neck, she felt a warm, thick liquid seeping through her fingers. Then an even sharper pain pierced through her the open folds of her overcoat and into her abdomen. Then another and another. Soon she was feeling shivery and lightheaded, her legs crumbling under the weight of her sudden agony and delirium. By the time she realized what was happening, she was on the ground, bleeding from a dozen entry wounds. It was like being on a runaway carousel, spinning wildly out of control.

This doesn't make any sense. This is all wrong. I have a life. I have a husband, a family, a job ... a husband ... Oh, Michael ... What ... have I done ... to you? What ...

Then the carousel slowed to a stop.

****

"Has the jury reached a verdict?"

"We have, your honor."

Surely it was a dream - or something akin to an out-of-body experience. From somewhere high above the courtroom, as if suspended from the stately, oak-paneled ceiling, Michael Gray looked down and saw himself seated in the front row, his stolid face drained of color, his dark haunted eyes transfixed on the venerable bench as this strange, surrealistic ritual reached its grim climax.

"Will the defendant rise and face the jury," a somber Judge Monahan instructed.

The accused, dressed in his best and only ill-fitting blue suit, slowly rose with his attorney, folded his hands at the waist and stoically turned toward his peers.

"Will the foreman read the verdict ..."

As the judge's voice faded, Michael's mind momentarily drifted into memory.

He was kissing Karen goodbye. Just a quick peck on her creamy soft cheek. He muttered something about having a good day, I'll see you tonight. She smiled the wistful smile of a knowing wife and lover, then pivoted gracefully on her heels. He watched her glide serenely down the street, then slowly turned away.

"We, the jury, find the defendant, Leon Edward Wendt ..."

Jasmine ... Michael suddenly remembered. That's what she had smelt like that morning.

"... not guilty."

The words slashed through Michael like a scalpel, gutting him from the pit of his stomach to the lump in his throat. Quickly the blood drained from his head, and for a moment he thought he would surely pass out. But he didn't, and when the room came into focus again he heard Judge Monahan sonorously declare, "The defendant is free to go."

The bang of the judge's gavel jarred Michael from his reverie and into the glaring light of stark reality. It was like a dungeon door slamming — a sound so frigid and final. Michael stared at

Wendt, absorbing the vile, chilling visage of his leering, pock-marked face, watching him as he triumphantly shook hands with his self-satisfied attorney and turned to face the courtroom crowd. Their eyes briefly meet. Michael caught his breath. The corner of Wendt's mouth curled into a smirk and he smugly looked away. Michael's impulse was to leap across the bar, tackle Wendt and pound his head into the stone floor until it oozed. But reason intervened. He knew he'd barely lay hands on the creep before he would be restrained. A guard was already at Wendt's side, prepared to escort him from the courtroom. Michael noticed the uniformed officer was wearing a sidearm. *Get up*, Michael told himself. *Get up while no one notices. Move discreetly toward the guard. Get alongside him, then go for the gun. Do it. Do it now before it's too late.* And, indeed, he did spring to his feet, ignoring his light-headedness.

He might have even taken a few steps forward. But again, his rational mind found fault with the plan. *Wait,* it advised. *Be patient. You know where he lives. You know where to find him. Wait.*

"Mr. Gray ..."

Michael wheeled around and was confronted by the state prosecutor, a balding nebbish in an overpriced suit and designer eyeglasses. "I'm ... I'm simply ... devastated," said the assistant district attorney with obligatory dismay.

"You told me it was an 'air-tight' case," Michael reminded him bitterly. "Those were your exact words."

"Yes, but ..."the prosecutor demurred, barely able to make eye contact. "We never anticipated there would be a ... technicality."

"What do you mean?" Michael demanded. "You had to have known the circumstances surrounding the search."

"There was no way to foresee that the evidence would be ruled inadmissible."

"Oh, really? So you're telling me that because the police were clumsy, my wife's murderer is free to walk the streets. Is that right?"

"Mr. Gray ..."

"Is that what you call justice?"

"Listen ..."

"I'm asking you ... *is that justice?*"

"I'm sorry."

"You're sorry," Michael muttered, struggling to control his emotions. "Well, I'm sorry, too. Sorry for *you*. Sorry for this lame excuse for a judicial system."

"Please, sir ..." the prosecutor murmured, placing his hand consolingly on Michael's shoulder.

"Excuse me," said Michael, shrugging him off. "I think I'm going to be sick." Michael pushed his way past the throng of courtroom spectators who were mulling in the aisle, past the reporters and other human obstacles that congested the hall outside, barely locating the nearest men's room stall before falling to his knees and gagging convulsively. However, nothing was regurgitated from his empty stomach. Instead, he knelt panting, his heart pounding, his smooth, pale hands trembling uncontrollably. In time the wave of nausea receded and his breathing subsided. There was a moment of stillness and sobering clarity. And then, comprehending his worst nightmare, he sobbed.

II

———————————

Eighteen months after his wife's death, Michael Gray was no closer to what some people quaintly referred to as "closure." Quite the contrary, he had only fallen deeper than ever into the abyss of loss and obsession. Awake, he would be haunted by Karen's memory virtually every second of every day, recalling minute details of their relatively brief but vivid history. Asleep, he would dream of her every night, restlessly pursuing her fleeting mirage through the shadowy labyrinth of his troubled mind. Sequestered in their midtown Manhattan apartment, he would linger for hours in her wardrobe closet, smelling her clothes, which he had refused to remove despite the tactful suggestions of sympathetic family and friends. Framed photographs of Karen still adorned tables and shelves, staring back at him with those tender blue eyes, and virtually every object, every trinket and memento in their apartment triggered inescapable recollections too precious to erase.

Alone in bed at night, Michael would even fantasize about their lovemaking, desperately pleasuring himself to climax with a painful shudder and weeping himself to sleep. How he missed the warmth of her flesh, the gentleness of her caress, the sweet taste of her lips. And yet, so many sensations lingered, so many images endured, so many terms of endearment echoed like pebbles tossed into a well.

It was not that Michael was in denial. He acknowledged and accepted Karen's death as an indisputable fact. Nevertheless, he still wore his gold wedding ring, as if subconsciously fearful that if he took it off, if only for a moment, she would be lost forever. He also clung to whatever belief offered the slightest hope. He had never subscribed to the wishful delusions of the religion into which he had been born, but now Michael sought comfort in the notion that there was indeed a heaven where one day he and Karen would be reunited forever. After all, it was one thing to lose a loved one and another to forget.

Weekly visits to the cemetery only made it more difficult to cope with his loss, yet Michael could not keep himself away. Even in the snowy depths of winter, he would make the somber pilgrimage to Queens to place fresh flowers on Karen's grave

She had loved lilacs and heather. If neither were in season, he would opt for white roses.

There were no silent prayers - Michael no longer had a need for a God who would have allowed such a tragedy to occur. Instead, he spoke to Karen aloud, briefing her on the week's events, bearing his tortured soul, reminding her of times they had spent together, of places they had gone, even the silly yet cherished pranks they had often played on each other.

There were many conflicting emotions to contend with - not merely grief. Michael felt somehow responsible for Karen's death, helpless and guilty. If it had to happen to one of them, why her? He should have protected her better. He should have made enough money for the two of them so that she didn't have to work. If she had been home that evening instead of alone on the streets of the city ... There was also a deep-seeded regret that, despite all evidence to the contrary, he had taken her for granted while she was alive. Surely, he could have been more attentive, more adoring, savoring every second they were together instead of pursuing his own selfish personal goals. He should have taken her to Paris as promised year after year. Now, it was too late. Now, the only goal was to get through another night without her.

Michael had his good days and bad days. The good days were those in which he was able to concentrate on his work and somehow avoid the tears. The bad days ranged from mere bouts of depression to a deeper and darker indulgence. He would stand before the bathroom mirror with a full bottle of seconal in his hand. He would study his reflection, wading through mixed emotions of guilt, self-loathing and unshakable despair. How simple and painless it would be to dispense with his usual prescription and bring a permanent end to his insomnia with a massive dose. Simple yet difficult for a man who no longer loved life yet still feared the unknown.

The very idea that Michael could ever love anyone again was as remote as the night was long. Not that he couldn't *have* a woman. There were plenty of available candidates in New York, certainly more than enough at the publishing company where he worked. The truth be told, being a 30-year old widower was quite an aphrodisiac. Scores of sympathetic females - single or divorced - were more than willing to help him forget and heal. But none, of course, compared to Karen in terms of beauty, style and grace.

No one ever could.

More than a few well-meaning people had suggested therapy - a victim's group, perhaps, if not a shrink. But Michael didn't see the point. He loathed the concept of talking one's way out of pain, of accepting the unacceptable and simply "moving on."

The only possible cure for his grief, he believed, was justice. And if the courts were unable or unwilling to provide it, there were always other means ...

****

Michael knew that Leon Wendt lived alone in a tenement on 111 Street between Broadway and Amsterdam Avenues. There was a vestibule and a lobby with a locked front door. There was also a service entrance to the building located in an alley further down the street. The metal door was often open, providing access to the building's basement and elevator. Wendt's apartment was on the sixth floor. One could easily pay him an unexpected visit, and hardly be noticed by his apathetic neighbors. One could simply knock on his door, pretending to be a delivery boy or the super or even a police detective - it's hard to recognize a real badge through a peephole.

Michael had actually visited Wendt's building on more than one occasion, at first standing across the street, observing the steady stream of tenants coming and going, then venturing into the vestibule to check the names on the buzzers until he found *L. Wendt - 6K.* He considered waiting there for someone to leave the building and pretending to be searching for his keys to gain entry. But he didn't have the nerve that day. Instead, he wandered outside and down the street until he discovered the unlocked service entrance.

Cautiously, he made his way through the dimly lit maze of the cavernous basement, chilled by its dank and shadowy silence, lurching past a utility annex and unoccupied laundry room to the building elevator. Fortunately, the lift bypassed the lobby and delivered him swiftly and inconspicuously to the sixth floor. There, he trod lightly down the black and white mosaic-tiled corridor until he reached a battered, metallic red door marked 6K.

It was mid-day. In all likelihood, Wendt was not at home. That is, if he had a job. Michael had no intention of knocking on his door to find out. He was merely content to stand there, imagining the surprised look on Wendt's face if he were to open the door only to be confronted by the Angel of Death. Michael wondered if Wendt would be so inclined as to smile if that were the case. Then, realizing where he was, how close he was and how easy it had been to get there, Michael's heart began to beat faster.

Gingerly, he leaned forward, tilted his head and listened for any sounds coming from the apartment. The stillness was forbidding. All Michael could hear was the faint rush of the wind in the nearby elevator shaft.

Suddenly, he heard the lock on the door to 6L turn. Startled, Michael bolted, scurrying away like a frightened mouse, reaching a nearby staircase just as the door open. He hastily proceeded down the spiraling exit route, floor after floor, until he reached the lobby and brushed past an indifferent old woman waiting for the elevator.

She scarcely glanced at him as he left the building and disappeared into the anonymity of the city streets.

Then, on one long weekend, Michael surprised his family and

friends by renting a car and taking a road trip to South Florida. Everyone took it as a sign that he had finally come to terms with his personal tragedy, that he was ready to begin enjoying life again.

What he did not tell anyone was that while in Fort Lauderdale he attended a gun show. There, armed with a hastily acquired concealed weapon's license, he bought himself a .9mm Beretta 92FS semi-automatic pistol. No sooner had he made the purchase than he was on his way back to New York, avoiding the scrutiny of airport security by driving all 1,200 miles. A lifelong gun control advocate, Michael nonetheless felt good about his new possession. Holding it in his hand gave him a sense of power and security - and the illusion that he was once again in control of his life.

But then April 21 arrived, the day that would have marked Karen and Michael's fifth wedding anniversary. He was unavoidably reminded of so many touchstones in their life together - their poignantly memorable wedding ceremony at his father's Connecticut country club, their modest but blissful honeymoon in Miami Beach, their exuberant celebrations with each holiday and job promotion, their chaotic but auspicious move from a studio apartment in Soho to a one-bedroom just east of Park Avenue, their fateful decision to start trying to have a baby … identifying Karen's body at the City Morgue, sitting in that courtroom day after day, and the cruel smile on Leon Wendt's face when he was acquitted.

Once again, Michael found himself standing on the edge of the abyss, gazing into the alluring darkness of oblivion. Only this time, he held a loaded weapon firmly in his grip. *Perhaps it wasn't Leon Wendt who needed to be punished,* he reasoned. Facing the mirror, Michael stared at his reflection, focusing on the dark, dilated pools of his sullen eyes, carelessly tucking the cold metal of the gun barrel under his unshaved chin. He closed his eyes and listened to the soft whisper of his shallow breathing. All that was required was a simple reflex action - one small step off the cliff and into the peaceful void. That's all it would take. In his mind's eye he saw Karen at the end of a long, illuminated corridor, her delicate, ageless smile beckoning. Remarkably unafraid, Michael held his breath, crooked his finger and pulled the trigger ...

10

But nothing happened. Bewildered, Michael opened his eyes and inspected the gun. Then he finally exhaled. *He had forgotten to remove the safety.* He let out a nervous titter, then pondered the miracle. Perhaps it was a sign. He wasn't meant to die - at least not today. He had a purpose for living on, a destiny to fulfill. Easing his grip, Michael studied the finely crafted contours of his awesome and noble weapon - and again recalled the heartless smile on Leon Wendt's face.

III

"You look terrible," Alan Davis remarked, setting aside his menu and regarding his best friend with grave concern.

"I haven't been sleeping that much," Michael confessed, glancing languidly around the restaurant.

"No shit," Alan muttered, regarding the rings under Michael's bloodshot eyes and the paleness of his complexion. He also noticed that several of Michael's cuticles had been gnawed to the point of bleeding and that he had lost a bit of weight. It reminded Alan of the time between Karen's death and the arrest of Leon Wendt, when he had spent many a long and dismal night consoling Michael. It was not a part of his life he wished to revisit. He held his tongue as long as he could, then spoke frankly. "Look, I know this is easy for me to say, but ... you've got to put it behind you."

Michael gently folded his hands on the table and humored Alan with a sad and weary smile. So, this would be another tiresome lunchtime discussion about dealing with *it*.

"You've got to be strong and ..."

"I want him dead," Michael bluntly declared, his forced smile abruptly vanishing.

Alan paused, unsure of what he had just heard.

"I want to piss on his grave," Michael coldly added.

"Hey ... I don't blame you," Alan agreed uneasily, knowing perfectly well of whom Michael was speaking. "I know how you feel. I really do."

"Yes, you know how I feel, but you don't *understand*," Michael insisted, leaning forward and looking deeply into Alan's serious brown eyes. "I want to *kill* him. I want to make him pay for what he did."

Alan glanced nervously at a nearby table, wishing Michael would lower his voice. "Of course you do," he replied quietly. "But you can't."

"Why not?"

"Well, for one thing, you don't have it in you. I mean, really ..."Alan scoffed, unraveling his napkin and placing it neatly on his lap. "And besides," he added sarcastically, "it happens to be illegal."

"Temporary insanity," said Michael without blinking an eye. "Hmm? *He* walked. Why can't I?"

Alan reached across the table and patted Michael's arm. "Come on. Let's not even discuss this."

"Why not?"

"Because it won't do us any good."

"You'd prefer to forget the whole thing, is that it? Just sweep it under the rug?"

"Of course not, Michael. It's just ..."

"What?"

"Taking the law into your own hands isn't the answer. It's not even an option. What do you want to do? Ruin your life?"

Michael let out a guffaw that drew the attention of several other diners. "My life *is* ruined," he wryly maintained. "What difference would it make?"

"You're wrong. You've got a lot to live for. You have a lot going for you," said Alan, grasping for straws. "You're ...you're young. You're bright. You're talented. You've got a great job and a promising career. You ... you ..."

"I have nothing," Michael declared. "Nothing, Alan. Let's face it – my ... so-called life ended when Karen died. The only thing that's keeping me alive is the need to see Leon Wendt punished. But that hasn't happened ... not yet."

"No, and it sucks. It really does," Alan admitted, wishing he were as good at dispensing personal advice as he was at financial planning. "But, Jesus, Michael ... obsessing over it is just going to torment you all the more."

"No offense, Alan, but what do you know about torment?"

Alan suppressed a smirk. He was tempted to enlighten Michael about the singular anguish of losing a spouse to infidelity and divorce. But again he refrained, realizing that it was difficult and pointless to argue with a man in as much pain as Michael. Besides, he knew he would feel the same way in his position. "What do you want?" he asked instead, immediately wishing he hadn't.

"I want justice," Michael told him.

"I meant, for lunch," said Alan, trying to inject a bit of levity into the conversation.

But Michael was in no laughing mood. "I want Leon Wendt to pay for what he did," he declared, slouching forward and jabbing the table with his pointed finger.

"He will," Alan insisted with little conviction. "Sooner or later, one way or another, the bastard is going to pay."

Michael leaned back in his chair and curled his lips into a cynical smile. "No, he won't. He'll just bide his time and keep his nose clean for awhile. Then he'll pick up where he left off. Free to kill again. It's in his nature. It's just a question of when. And next time, it'll be someone else's wife ... or sister or daughter. Only he'll be more careful. He'll have a better alibi, less evidence. He won't rely on a technicality to beat the rap. Mark my words – he'll get away with it ... again." Choking on his words, struggling to hold back his tears, Michael bit his lip and grimly intoned, "He has to be stopped. *He has to pay.*"

Suddenly, a perky waitress appeared at their table. "Hi, my name is Tamara. Can I start you gentlemen off with a drink?"

"Scotch on the rocks," said Alan, regaining his composure and forcing a smile.

"And for you, sir?"

"Just water, please," Michael muttered, not even bothering to make eye contact.

"I'll be right back," Tamara promised, then darted off.

It was obvious from the anxious look in Alan's eyes that he was beginning to take Michael all too seriously. "Man ... you're freakin' me out," he laughed apprehensively, running his hand through his thinning black hair, or what was left of it.

"Don't sweat it," Michael replied. "It's not your problem."

"Yeah, well, I don't know about that. Just promise me you won't do anything foolish," Alan practically pleaded.

"I can't promise you anything," Michael replied.

"What do you plan to do, anyway?" Alan asked sarcastically. " Shoot him?"

Michael simply stared.

"Come on," Alan scoffed. "Get real."

"This is as real as it gets," Michael assured him. "Shoot him, stab him, push him in front of a train – what difference does it make? As long as he dies, I don't care how it gets done. You think I don't have it in me?" Michael reached into his jacket pocket and slapped a slug onto the table. Dumbstruck, Alan stared at the bullet, then looked directly into Michael's steely eyes. "Watch me," said Michael.

The determined tone of his voice sent a shiver through Alan. He had known Michael for 13 years, ever since they were freshmen in college. If there was anything he had learned about him in all that time, it was that once Michael set his mind to a task he always saw it through. Alan agreed that Leon Wendt was guilty as sin and that he deserved a punishment worse than life imprisonment. After all, it was Alan who introduced Michael to Karen, Alan who had served as best man at their wedding. He, too, had loved and admired and wept for Karen. It was a cold, dark day when Leon Wendt walked out of that courtroom as a free man, and not only did it anger Alan but it drove a knife through his heart to see what it was doing to his friend. Once carefree, witty and just plain fun to be around, Michael had become a morose and distant shell of his former self. For that alone Wendt deserved a lethal injection. But what Michael was suggesting was more than dangerous – it was self-destructive. And Alan didn't want to lose both of them – not Karen *and* Michael. Usually cool and calm in a crisis, he nevertheless felt helpless and afraid in the face of his friend's vengeful sense of purpose.

"Okay," said Alan. "I believe you. Now, please ... put that away."

Michael palmed the bullet and returned it to his pocket.

Alan searched in vain for their waitress. He needed that drink. "Tell me something, Michael," he said after a long silence.

"What?"

"When was the last time I asked you for a favor?"

Michael shrugged.

"Will you do one for me now?" asked Alan.

"It depends on the favor."

"Assuming you're determined to follow through on your ... plan, I'd like you to hold off for awhile."

"How long is awhile?"

"At least a week."

"Alan ..."

"Please."

"What difference will a week make? I'm not going to change my mind. I'm not going to cool off, if that's what you think."

"No. I know. I just want you to give *me* a little time."

"To do what?"

"To come up with an alternative."

Michael shook his head. "There is no alternative. No simple solution. No easy way out."

"A week," Alan requested.

"I don't want you to be involved," Michael insisted. "This is my responsibility."

"*Please*," Alan implored.

Michael brushed a strand of hair from his forehead and sighed. "Seven days," he finally conceded.

"Seven days," Alan repeated, already considering a more viable solution.

IV

Cynthia Porter had a way of turning heads. Tall, blonde and blue-eyed, she was arguably the most attractive employee at Paragon Books, Inc. But she was also one of the most savvy and accomplished, responsible for polishing no less than seven *New York Times* bestsellers – fiction, no less – during her tenure. A magnum cum laude graduate of Sarah Lawrence College, she had come a long way in a relatively short time, starting her career at Paragon two days after graduation and vaulting from assistant copy editor to copy editor to senior editor in a mere three years.

Of course, it didn't hurt that she was young, unattached and had a fine figure that even tasteful business attire could not disguise. She had received more than her share of unsolicited attention from men, single and married, in and out of the office. Yet she lived alone, slept alone and hadn't seen a man naked in at least a year. It was not that she was disinterested in the dating scene or a slave to her professional ambitions – she simply had her standards.

It was therefore not surprising to Cynthia that she was secretly drawn to Michael Gray. Like a character in one of the novels that frequently crossed her desk, he possessed all the qualities she found alluring in a man – intelligence, sensitivity, discretion and a certain air of mystery. Also, there was something tragically romantic about his well-concealed but unmistakable grief, something noble about his undying devotion to his late wife. He was that most enticing of challenges – a seemingly unattainable man she respected and admired from afar, perhaps a man she could learn to love – if only he knew that she existed.

Of course, he did know that she existed. They shared the same wing of the 21st floor – he, the executive vice president, ensconced in a corner office, and she, the up-and-coming senior editor, located four doors down the hall. If they didn't run into each other at the coffee machine or in the research library, they would see each other at weekly editorial staff meetings and the occasional office social event. On occasions, they would be teamed on certain projects requiring Cynthia to run manuscripts by Michael for his input, review and/or approval. But that was the extent of their relationship – until one afternoon when Cynthia decided it was time to take a more aggressive approach with the aloof Mr. Gray.

"Hi," she smiled, poking her head into the open doorway of his office.

Michael looked up from his desk, peering over a pair of reading glasses. "Hi," he replied sheepishly.

"Got a minute?" Cynthia asked, entering the room before he had a chance to respond.

"I suppose."

Cynthia glanced about, then declared, "You win the prize."

"How's that?"

"Yours is the most uncluttered, organized desk at Paragon."

"Oh, really? What do I win?" Michael quipped, playing along.

"Hmm," Cynthia hesitated, thinking of a witty comeback. "More work?" she offered, handing him the small stack of fresh manuscripts she had tucked under her arm.

"Gee, thanks," he remarked, accepting the gift. "Remind me to provide some positive comments for your next performance review."

Cynthia crossed her arms behind her, unconsciously calling attention to her ample, jutting bosom. Respectfully, Michael maintained eye contact. "How are things going?" she asked, brushing her thighs against the edge of Michael's desk.

"Things?"

"Yeah ... things." They both knew what she was alluding to.

"Okay, I guess," Michael sighed, putting on his bravest face. "Some days are a bit rainy ... and some are just partly cloudy."

"I hear you."

"And how are 'things' going for you?" Michael queried, unable to avoid noticingthat the top three buttons of Cynthia's white blouse were open – spotting a hint of cleavage.

"I could use a social life," she conceded, briefly toying with a strand of hair. "But otherwise I can't complain."

There was a long pause in the conversation as they ran out of clever repartee. It was Cynthia who was forced to break the silence. "Look," she leveled, tossing back her golden locks, "I haven't read *Cosmo* in awhile and I don't know if it's necessarily the politically correct thing to do in this post-feminist age, but ... I was wondering if you'd like to join me for a drink after work."

Michael looked like a deer frozen in someone's headlights. "Tonight?"

"Or anytime," Cynthia hastened to suggest, recognizing that wavering look on his face, as if he were searching for a valid excuse to decline the invitation.

"I'm not much of a drinker," Michael demurred.

"Well, neither am I to tell you the truth," Cynthia confessed. "But it is a good way to get to know someone better. Don't you think? I mean, we don't have to share a whole bottle of Bacardi. You could have a Shirley Temple if it suits you – I won't think you're a sissy."

"That's a relief."

"So what do you think?"

Michael looked away, squirming in his chair. "I think you have no idea what poor company I can be."

"Well, I have my suspicions," Cynthia teased, pleased that her remark elicited an impulsive smile. "Listen, I'm no bargain, either," she added for good measure.

Taking a deep breath, Michael inadvertently caught a whiff of her enticing perfume. For a moment, he actually entertained the notion of cocktails and chitchat – and perhaps more. He was about to accept, but then happened to glance at the framed photo of Karen on the corner of his desk. The wind in his sails abruptly subsided. "Thanks just the same," he muttered, "but ..."

Not ready, thought Cynthia, trying not to let her disappointment show. "How about a raincheck?" she suggested, trying not to sound too aggressive or, worse, desperate.

"Sure," Michael nodded with a faint smile. The old raincheck. Did anyone ever make good on one?

"Fine," Cynthia nodded, backing away. "Well, I've got a few deadlines. So ... I'll see ya' around."

"Yeah."

Michael watched her leave, then swiveled in his chair to face the window. His view of midtown Manhattan was the envy of Editorial, a complex vista of skyscrapers, thoroughfares and skyline that served him well in moments of intense reflection. There had been another reason why he declined Cynthia's invitation. He knew that by this time next week, he would be in a holding cell, probably warding off the advances of fellow inmates, awaiting arraignment for the murder of Leon Wendt. A pity about the consequences – his career, his freedom, his finances, his prospects with Cynthia Porter or any other woman, for that matter. But that's the way the cookie crumbles. Still, it was better than spending the rest of his life knowing that Karen's killer was out there, free to come and go as he pleased, laughing and drinking and living a long, long life.

Thinking about it all just upset Michael. He called it quits at 5:15, instead of his usual 7:30 or 8:00, and picked up Szechuan on his way home. Later that night he resisted indulging in his usual routine of watching the wedding video and thumbing through the eight photo albums he and Karen had accumulated. There was no need for that torture this evening.

Instead, Michael found a small degree of solace in the ritual of inspecting his gun, running his fingertips along its cool, sleek barrel, unloading and reloading its magazine in rapid succession, curling his fingers around its thick, solid handle. Although his experience with discharging the weapon had been limited to a few recent sessions at a local firing range – and hardly with results that would classify him as a marksman – he had every confidence that he could handle the firearm at close range and rid the world of Leon Wendt. That is, if he could actually pull the trigger.

Michael knew it was one thing to hold a gun in his hand, take aim and imagine blowing his wife's murderer away. It was another thing, however, to cross the line between intent and action – to *kill*. The more Michael stared at the Beretta, the more doubtful he became. *You don't have it in you*, Alan had told him. What if he was right? Despite all the pain and anger and bloodlust, that was the thing that frightened Michael most of all.

V

Leon Wendt was in a deep sleep, floating like a cloud over a range of snow-capped mountains, miles away from the big, bad city and the dark, cold Hudson River. He was flying, would you believe, flying without wings or strings. And it felt so natural that he was certain this was real, so simple. Why hadn't he ever done this before? Just take off and fly …

But all of a sudden, a sound like thunder split the sky. No, not thunder – something worse. A shrill that electrified his senses and sent him plummeting to Earth. Downward he descended, tumbling as he fell, building speed at an alarming rate. But before Wendt landed, he abruptly awoke, gasping for breath, his heart pounding in his chest.

Disoriented, he looked around. He was sitting on a couch, his couch, in his living room. It was the middle of the day. A window was open. He could hear the familiar sounds of the city traffic outside. It was a far, far cry from floating like a cloud over snow-capped mountains.

The bell rang again, once more jarring him to alertness. Instinctively, Wendt rose to his feet and trudged toward the intercom in the hallway by the door to his apartment. He pressed a button and grunted, "Yeah?"

"Hey, man," replied a voice that was vaguely familiar. "It's Ray."

"Who?"

"Ray! Ray!" the visitor impatiently barked. "Buzz me in, *bandajo*!"

Wendt hesitated, wondering why Ray was paying him a visit. He didn't owe him any money. They didn't have any unfinished business. They hadn't even seen each other for weeks. *Whatever*, Wendt thought and pressed the button long enough for Ray to gain access to the building.

Massaging the back of his neck, Wendt set about the task of straightening up the living room. Scattered clothing was gathered and tossed on a pile in the bedroom, sections of newspaper were snatched and stuffed in the nearest trash bin, and day old dishes and plates were relocated to the kitchen sink just as Ray knocked on the door.

"Hey, man," Wendt greeted him at the threshold.

"Hey," Ray nodded, entering the apartment without waiting for an invitation.

"Wassup?" asked Wendt, closing the door.

"Not much," said Ray, turning to face him. "Just thought I'd drop by. See how things are going." He was wearing his usual street clothes – dark blue ski cap, army camouflage jacket, black chinos and a pair of white sneakers. He was a short but stocky Latino whose bushy black mustache always contained bits of his latest meal. Today, it was crumbs from a hero sandwich.

"I don't owe you no money, do I?" Wendt wondered aloud.

"No, no," Ray replied. "Like I said, I just thought I'd see you."

"Ah-huh," Wendt grunted, doubting Ray would ever drop by unannounced just to shoot the breeze. That wasn't what their relationship was all about. "Well, you want to sit down?" he asked, motioning toward the couch.

"No," said Ray, keeping his hands in his pockets and flexing on his toes.

"You want something to drink?" Wendt offered.

Ray shook his head. "I'm cool. Not gonna' stay that long."

"Yeah, well, I need a Red Bull," Wendt admitted, heading for the kitchen.

Hangover, Ray surmised, surveying the shabby living room with a critical eye. He didn't notice any drug paraphernalia, but it was obvious from the condition of the place that not much had changed.

"Sure I can't get you anything?" asked Wendt, returning with his drink in hand.

Ray cocked his head. "You don't look so good," he observed.

"I was sleeping," said Wendt, taking a swig. "That's all."

"Yeah? You sure?"

"What do you mean, am I sure? I was sleeping."

"You're not strung out?"

"Uh-uh," Wendt emphatically replied. "I kicked it."

"Yeah, right," smiled Ray.

"I did," Wendt insisted. "No more shit for me."

"I've heard that one before."

"Look, I got a job. They test me every month. If I so much as eat a poppy bagel, I could get canned."

"I hear you, man," Ray humored him. Though there are ways to get around that drug test shit."

"I'm not taking no chances."

"Too bad," said Ray, slowly removing one of his hands from his jacket pocket. "Cause I got a new supply." He produced a small plastic bag containing a powdery white substance. "One hundred percent Colombian, man. I could give you a little taste for free."

Wendt stared at the bag, then at Ray. "I don't need no taste, man," he told him. "I need to keep my ass out of prison."

Ray's smile became a smirk. "Yeah, well, you dodged a big bullet last time, didn't you?" he remarked.

Wendt wanted to wipe the smirk off his face, but you didn't mess with a guy like Ray. "That was bullshit, man," he contended. "I didn't kill that bitch."

"Of course not," said Ray playfully. "You wouldn't do a thing like that. Even if you was strung out."

Suddenly, Wendt's patience was running out. "Look, man. I got a lot to do today," he said, taking another big gulp and finishing the can of Red Bull.

Ray glanced around the room and returned the plastic bag to his pocket. "Yeah, I can see that. Well, if you change your mind …"

"I don't think so," said Wendt, crushing the can in his fist.

Ray walked past him and toward the door. "Like I said … *if* you change your mind, you know where to find me." And then he showed him out.

Alone, Wendt tossed the crushed can out the living room window and listened as it clanged against the sidewalk below. He looked around the room at his torn and tattered used furniture, at the water stain on the ceiling and the peeling plaster on the walls. Was it his imagination, or was the room getting smaller every day? Sick and tired of the sounds of the city, he closed the window and drew down the shade. But he could still hear the police and ambulance sirens, the horns of a thousand taxicabs, and the overblown bass of a hip-hop song on some gangsta's car stereo. To drown it all out, he turned on his TV and tuned in some game show. Parked on his couch, he gazed at the tube until he feel back asleep, trying in vain to learn how to fly again.

VI

It wasn't like Alan to call so late at night. But then he knew that Michael wouldn't be asleep and what he had to tell him was too important to wait until the morning. "It's me," he said, practically whispering into the phone. "I've got something for you."

Michael pressed the mute button on his television remote and silenced Bill Mahr's monologue. "What is it?" he asked.

"A solution to your problem," Alan replied.

Michael sat up in bed. "I'm listening."

"I made some inquiries," Alan cryptically explained. "As it turns out, a friend of a friend knows a guy who can help you." He sounded as if he were talking in code, as if worried that his phone was being bugged.

"I don't follow you," said Michael.

Alan sighed. "I'm telling you that I found the way to handle your problem. The *right way*."

Michael caught his breath. He wasn't sure what his friend was suggesting, but he was beginning to get an inkling.

Alan wasn't one to mince words. "What I'm saying is … why risk everything by doing it yourself, when you can leave it to a professional?"

Of course, Michael realized. Why hadn't he thought of that himself? God knows, he had seen this sort of thing in movies and on television a million times. It *was* the way to get it done – and get away with it. "Are you sure about this?" he asked, feeling a sudden rush of titillating anxiety.

"I'm totally serious," Alan earnestly intoned.

"Okay ... How does it work?"

"All you have to do is make a phone call."

"Who am I calling? What's his name?"

"That I don't know," said Alan.

"What do you mean, you don't know?"

"I wasn't privy to that particular detail. I mean, anonymity is essential. Does it matter?"

"I guess not."

"All I've got is a beeper number. You call it and he calls you back. Then, you take it from there."

"Uh-huh. And tell me again – where did you get this ... reference?"

"From someone who doesn't know you and, more importantly, doesn't know that *I* know you. The fewer people involved, the better."

Alan did have his connections from all walks of life – from legitimate entrepreneurs to small-time tax evaders to middle management in certain "family businesses." He was the guy you went to for tickets to sold-out performances or the seventh game of the Stanley Cup finals, or for a reliable mechanic, or for electronic equipment at wholesale prices.

"You're not bullshitting me, are you?" Michael wondered aloud. "You know, jerking me around in order to buy some time and prevent me from doing what I had planned to do."

"Don't be ridiculous," Alan chided.

"Because this is serious stuff."

"Believe me, I know."

Michael ran his hand through his hair and sighed deeply into the phone. "Why are you doing this for me?"

"Why? *Why?* Because you're my best friend, you crazy *shmuck*. Because I don't want to see you do anything foolish – like spend the rest of your life behind bars. If your mind is set on revenge ..."

"It is," Michael confirmed.

"Then this is a more viable alternative," Alan contended. "Costly, perhaps, but more viable."

"I don't care about the money."

"Ah-huh. But are you sure you can live with it?"

"Oh, yeah," Michael assured him. "I can live with it."

"Then in that case ... have you got a pen handy?"

"Hold on a second," said Michael, hastily rummaging through the drawer of his nightstand. "Go ahead, give me the number."

After jotting it down on the back of a magazine, Michael took a deep breath. "Thanks, Alan," he said.

"Don't mention it."

"I'll call tomorrow and then let you know how it went."

"Don't bother," Alan advised. "I don't want to know any of the details. Besides, you should keep it totally confidential. Just between you and Mr. X. Tell no one else. Not even your pet. Understand?"

"I don't have a pet."

"Good. And if anybody questions me, I won't know what the hell they're talking about. Are we on the same page?"

"As always."

"Fine. Now get some sleep. You've got work in the morning, for Christ's sake."

But Michael couldn't sleep. He was too excited. After he hung up the phone, he turned off the television and got out of bed. He slipped into a bathrobe and a pair of slippers, popped open a bottle of Chardonnay and poured himself a tall glass. Restless, he stepped out onto his terrace for some fresh air and introspection. Gazing at the city skyline, he sipped his wine and was reminded of the many times he and Karen had shared this view. She loved the sight of towering skyscrapers illuminating the night, the endless vistas that spanned north and west, the stars and the moon and the endless twinkle of a jet airliner in the distance. "You're with me, baby," he murmured, closing his eyes. "You're still with me."

When Michael opened his eyes, the scene was unchanged, but he was unmistakably alone. Nevertheless, he allowed his mind to consider a new world of hitherto inconceivable possibilities. A cool evening breeze seemed to blow away the cobwebs. It was as if a great weight had been lifted from his weary shoulders. For the first time in a long time, it felt better – if not good – to be alive. Finally, there was a ray of hope.

VII

It was an interesting dilemma – whether to call the beeper number from the office or from home. Michael was anxious to make contact as soon as possible, yet feared missing the return call if he were in a meeting or if he merely stepped away from his desk for a moment. It was not the kind of return call one wanted recorded on one's voice mail. Also, there was a question of privacy. How could he discuss taking out a contract on a man's life on an unsecured line or within earshot of the rest of the staff? He couldn't afford to be hasty – or careless, for that matter. He would just have to be patient, cunningly so, and play it safe.

Although preoccupied for eight interminable work hours, Michael managed to refrain until he got home before picking up the phone and pressing the seven digits that could irreversibly alter his life. Then it was just a matter of waiting. He tried to focus on household chores, writing checks and channel surfing. But instead he found himself pacing the apartment, drifting from room to room like a lovesick schoolgirl waiting to be asked to the prom. He had skipped dinner, too nervous to eat. All he could nimble on were his throbbing cuticles. *Why hasn't he called,* Michael wondered fretfully. *Is he too busy whacking people to pick up a phone?*

After two nerve-racking hours without a response, Michael decided to call the number again. But just as he reached for the phone, it rang. Startled, he jerked back his hand, as if avoiding the fangs of a venomous cobra. The phone rang again, seemingly louder and more insistent. Regaining his composure, Michael lifted the receiver.

"Hello?"

There was dead silence on the line for several long seconds. Then a deep, unsettlingly indifferent voice intoned, "You called me."

"Y-yes," Michael awkwardly acknowledged. "Yes, I did. I ... I was given your number by a friend."

There was a long pause as the caller awaited further explanation. When he realized that none was forthcoming, he drolly replied, "And?"

Michael swallowed inaudibly, took a deep breath and pressed on. "I'm in need of ... a special service. I understand that you might be able to help me."

"Possibly."

"Do you want me to tell you about it over the phone?"

"No. I know why you called."

"You ... you do?" Michael tensely murmured, shifting the receiver from his left ear to his right.

"We'll talk about it in person," said the stranger. "Just give me your name."

"My name?"

"Uh-huh."

"It's Michael ... Michael Gray. May I ask *your* name?"

"That's not important, Mr. Gray."

"It isn't?"

"Just meet me tomorrow night at Angelo's."

"Angelo's?"

" It's a restaurant in the Village. Do you know where it is?"

"I'm afraid I don't," Michael confessed, somewhat taken aback by the caller's chilly, condescending manner.

"It's on Sullivan Street, two blocks south of Washington Square Park. You can't miss it."

"What time do you want me there?"

"Nine o'clock."

"How will I recognize you?"

"You won't."

"Well ... how will *you* recognize *me*?" asked Michael.

"That's easy," the caller dryly replied. "You'll be the guy looking for somebody."

"Yeah, well ... I'll be wearing a tan raincoat. How's that?"

"Whatever."

"Okay, then. Tomorrow at ..." Suddenly, Michael heard a click. "Hello? Hello? The bastard hung up on me," he muttered incredulously.

Nevertheless, Michael was pleased that he and Mr. X had a date. Judging purely by his voice and attitude, the mysterious hitman was the genuine article – cool, calm and collected yet a real badass, a no-nonsense character who was obviously as discreet as he was probably merciless. Poor, pitiful Leon Wendt – if he only knew the world of trouble that awaited him. Psyched, Michael gently placed the receiver on its cradle. This was going to be easier than he thought.

****

Due to unexpectedly heavy traffic and an uncharacteristically lethargic cab driver, Michael arrived at Angelo's ten minutes late for his appointment. "I'm meeting someone," he explained to the hostess, an attractive if corpulent woman whose heavy eye makeup only succeeded in making her look much older than she was. She graced him with an obligatory smile, yet there was a hint of suspicion in her eyes. Or was it merely Michael's imagination? Come to think of it, hadn't the cab driver glanced at him in the rear view mirror once too often?

While unbuttoning his raincoat, Michael proceeded into the dining room and slowly made his way toward the rear of the spacious restaurant. As he passed each table, he glanced at the diners. He was searching for a burly, surly man who was eating alone, but all he noticed were silent couples and gabby quartets, all of whom warily returned his curious gaze. Was it that obvious? Did they all know why he was there? How skittish and paranoid had he become? It was one thing to feel guilty after the fact. But during premeditation? Wandering aimlessly about the room, he began to wonder whether Mr. X had even bothered to show up – or if he had left in indignation when Michael failed to arrive on time.

Then a deep, hauntingly familiar voice seemed to tap him on the shoulder. "Mr. Gray ..."

Michael paused, slowly turned and focused on a man sitting in a corner booth. He was wearing a black leather jacket, a white silk shirt, a pair of designer blue jeans and sleek black boots. Hunched with his elbows on the table, he took a deep drag on a European cigarette and gracefully exhaled. "You're late," he said through a shroud of blue smoke.

"Sorry," Michael apologized, tentatively approaching his table. "I ... I was detained."

"Have a seat."

Michael slid into the booth, facing Mr. X but finding it difficult at first to make eye contact with him. "I hope you weren't waiting too long," he said.

"Long enough," his contact replied dryly.

Michael self-consciously glanced over his shoulder and scanned the neighboring tables. "Is it safe to talk here?"

"As safe as it gets. Just keep your voice down."

"I haven't done anything like this before," Michael timidly admittedly.

"Obviously," Mr. X muttered, taking another puff and blowing the smoke in Michael's direction.

"I just mean ... I don't know where to start."

"Why don't you start by giving me a name," Mr. X suggested. "An address would be helpful, too – though not absolutely necessary."

Before Michael could respond, a perky waitress in a ruffled white shirt and black bow tie and slacks suddenly appeared. "Good evening, gentlemen," she chimed. "Can I start you off with a drink? Your usual, Butch?" she asked, addressing Mr. X with a friendly tone connoting familiarity.

He shot her a disapproving glance, not because she was intruding but because she had inadvertently divulged his nickname. But then, suspecting that Michael hadn't taken note of it, Butch flashed a tolerant smile and dismissively replied, "We're okay, sweetheart. Maybe later."

"I guess you're a regular here," Michael surmised as the waitress attended to another table.

Butch ignored the comment and took another puff. "What have you got for me?" he asked impatiently.

That was obviously Michael's cue. He reached into his raincoat, removed a slip of paper and pushed it across the table. While Butch reviewed the information, Michael took visual inventory. He had thick, prematurely gray hair and striking Mediterranean features – a high, unfurrowed brow, a finely chiseled beak of a nose, a slightly jutting jaw with a cleft in his chin and an olive complexion. He was probably Italian-American, but possibly Greek. He didn't really sound like your run-of-the-mill wiseguy, but his accent was distinctly New York metropolitan. Judging by the condition of his relatively creaseless face, he was in his early to mid-forties. He also had a trim yet solid upper body, no doubt the product of regular workouts. His hands were large and thick, but relatively smooth, his fingernails freshly manicured. He also had an obvious affinity for gold: He wore a simple gold chain around his neck, a gold and diamond-encrusted ring on his left pinkie, an authentic gold Rolex on his wrist, and kept a gold cigarette case on the table. That seemed to sum him up until Butch tilted his head and Michael noticed something else – a nasty scar that ran diagonally along the left side of his neck. Someone had apparently gone for the jugular and failed. Michael shuddered to think what had happened to the other guy.

Then Butch casually reached into his breast pocket and removed a shiny gold cigarette lighter. With a single flick, he ignited the piece of paper and deposited it in his ashtray. As it burned to a cinder, he trained his piercing blue eyes on Michael and blew a narrow stream of smoke across the table. "No problem," he said with an air of utter boredom and supreme confidence.

"Don't you want to know why?" asked Michael.

"I couldn't care less," said Butch.

"Well, I want to tell you," Michael insisted.

"To ease your conscience?"

"He deserves it."

Butch shrugged indifferently and drew on his cigarette. "If you say so."

"He attacked and murdered my wife," Michael declared.

Butch didn't even seem to be listening, preoccupied with that cigarette and his own random thoughts.

"He left her bleeding to death ..." Michael bitterly intoned. "... like she was nothing." Still no reaction. "He was acquitted because of a legal technicality. Now he's out there, walking the streets."

"Not for long," Butch quipped, tapping his ashes and smoothly exhaling smoke through his nose.

It was precisely what Michael wanted to hear – the unflinching assurance that, at long last, justice would be served. And yet, there was something about Butch's frosty, strictly business attitude that he found disturbing. It was purely mercenary, detached and devoid of emotion. In fact, it reminded Michael of Leon Wendt's icy, unfeeling demeanor.

"How do you intend to ..." Michael began to ask, pausing as another waitress passed their table en route to the kitchen. He waited until she was gone, then asked in a quieter voice, "How do you intend to do it?"

"That's not your concern," said Butch, tapping his cigarette on the edge of the ashtray. "The less you know about the how, when and where, the more likely it'll go off without a hitch. But I can promise you it'll be efficient. In fact, you won't even feel as if you were involved."

Fair enough, thought Michael. But there was another delicate matter that needed to be discussed. "What's this going to cost me?" he asked.

"How much have you got?" Butch replied deadpan. A few beats later, he smiled. "Just kidding. Twenty thousand. Ten before and ten after. In cash, of course."

Michael bit his lip. "*Ten* thousand? In advance?"

"In cash," Butch repeated. "That's my minimum fee for dealing with insignificant scumbags who ordinarily wouldn't be worth the effort. Is there a problem with that?"

"Well, no," Michael demurred. "It's just ... how do I know you won't ..."

"Take the ten grand and disappear?"

"Not that I don't trust you," Michael hastened to add. "It's just ..."

"Hey," said Butch sternly, "you can't afford *not* to trust me. From what I'm hearing, I'm all you got. I'm your fuckin' last resort, *Mr. Gray.* Now do you want this done ... or not?"

"Of course I want it done ..."

"Then listen carefully," Butch demanded, stamping out his cigarette.

"Tomorrow, go to your bank and withdraw $21,000."

"Why twenty-one?" asked Michael.

"You're not listening to me," Butch chided with simmering displeasure. He deliberately stared at Michael for several seconds before continuing. "Stash $10,000 where no one will find it. I'll call you tomorrow night and tell you where to meet me to hand over the deposit. Are we clear so far?"

Michael nodded.

"Then I want you to take a few days off," Butch instructed. "Go on a little trip with the remaining $1,000."

"A trip? Where am I going?"

"I would suggest Atlantic City. Stay at a nice hotel. Order room service. Sign for it. Show your face to as many people as possible. And while you're at it, spend lots of time in the casinos. Feed a few slot machines. Flirt with a cocktail waitress."

"Why?"

"To establish an alibi."

"An alibi?"

"You probably won't need one – depending on how smoothly I get this job done. But if the police get suspicious as to why the guy acquitted of your wife's murder suddenly met with unfortunate circumstances, you may need to prove that you were out of town at the time. And you'll have to explain why you made such a substantial withdrawal from your account recently. If they want to know where all the money went, you can tell them you lost it gambling. The casino's security videotapes will substantiate your story."

"And the other $10,000? The money I hid?"

"If the heat is on, we'll wait until it cools off. Then, when the proverbial coast is clear, I'll call you to arrange a drop-off."

Michael didn't know what was more chilling – the idea of paying someone to commit murder or Butch's effortless ingenuity. "Okay," he agreed, taking a deep breath. "Is that it?"

"Unless you have some more questions," Butch replied, stashing his cigarette case in his vest pocket.

Michael shook his head. "No ... I don't think so."

"Good," said Butch. "The less said, the better." And without saying another word – not so much as a goodbye – he slid out of the booth and casually walked out of the restaurant.

"Nice talking to you," Michael muttered, watching him head for the door.

A bit shaken from the encounter, Michael took a deep cleansing breath, only to trigger a cough. He looked disapprovingly at the ashtray on the table. Although Butch had crushed his cigarette, it still smoldered, its lingering fumes making him want to gag. He only hoped he was doing the right thing.

The perky waitress reappeared with pad and pen in hand. "Can I get you anything, hon?" she asked.

"How about some arsenic?" Michael muttered.

"Excuse me?"

"Scotch on the rocks," he ordered. "Please."

VIII

The morning after his meeting with Butch, Michael awoke with a mild hangover. One drink had led to another the night before, and the cab ride home was just a blur. Consciously, he had rationalized his imbibing as a way of celebrating the impending demise of Leon Wendt. Subconsciously, it was because he had misgivings about the hastily sanctioned arrangement.

Nevertheless, after a bracing shower and a few strong cups of caffeinated coffee, Michael went about his business as usual. He arrived at the office at 8:45 a.m., rolled up his sleeves and diligently focused on his work for the next few hours. Promptly at noon, however, he dropped everything and reluctantly headed for the nearest branch of his personal bank.

Although he understood the need for an alibi, Michael thought the Atlantic City ruse was too uncharacteristic of him. Why would an executive editor at Paragon Books suddenly feel the urge to withdraw $21,000 from his life savings and head for the casinos – coincidentally, just days before his wife's alleged killer is found dead? Besides, the idea of carrying around that much cash made him nervous. Surely, there was a safer, easier way to establish a more credible alibi.

So Michael merely withdrew $10,000 from his savings account. Since Butch hadn't specified whether he wanted the cash in small bills, Michael requested five one thousand dollar bills, a stack of hundreds, and several fifties and twenties. Unusually circumspect, the bank teller asked him to press his account access code on a keypad. Patiently complying, Michael tried to look as nonchalant as possible. Of course, he accidentally pressed an eight, instead of a nine, and apologetically had to repeat the process. No big deal. After the transaction was completed, he stashed the cash in his leather briefcase, discreetly returned to his office and kept the money under lock and key in the file drawer of his desk.

As expected, Butch called Michael at home later that night. "Have you got the deposit?" he asked amid background noise that made it obvious he was calling from a public phone.

"Yes," Michael replied.

"Good. Meet me at Columbus Circle in twenty minutes."

"Now? Tonight?"

"Yeah. What's the problem?"

"Well ... I don't have the money with me," Michael explained. "It's in my office."

"So? Go and get it," said Butch.

"I can't. I mean ... it's late. We've got a security guard in the lobby. I'd have to sign in. It may look suspicious – showing up at eleven o'clock to get something out of my office. You know what I mean?"

Butch sighed. "You do have the money, though?"

"Yes, yes. I've got the money."

"Where's your office?"

"Madison and 58th Street."

"Then meet me at 12:30 tomorrow at the fountain across the street from the Plaza."

"The Plaza Hotel?"

"That's the one. And bring the money."

"Yes, of course. I'll bring the money."

And with an abrupt click, Butch was gone.

Michael scarcely slept that night, tossing and turning to the wail of police and ambulance sirens, the faint but unmistakable jabbering on his neighbor's television through the bedroom wall, and the fearful murmurs of certain voices in his head. And when he finally did drift off to sleep, he was plagued with disturbing dreams. The only one he recalled was a recurring one in which he inherited a big old house in a deep dark forest. Elegantly decorated, the mansion was several stories tall, each floor containing an intriguing surprise. In this particular dream, there was a spacious, though empty, ballroom on the ground floor with mirrored walls, huge crystal chandeliers suspended from the ceiling and dead leaves strewn across a marble floor. Beyond a pair of French doors was an adjacent solarium filled with exotic orchids and lush, overflowing vegetation. But Michael would wander elsewhere, from kitchen to dining room to sitting room to parlor, through intersecting corridors that seemed endless but ultimately led to a winding carpeted staircase. Alone, he would climb to the second floor where he would find a music room, unfurnished but for a grand piano with a ticking metronome perched on its narrow desk. Through a bay window he would watch as daylight slowly faded, compelling him to press on. Without moving he was transported to the next floor, to the threshold of a mysterious library with a flaming hearth that cast ghostly shadows on stacks of rare, unread volumes embedded in towering bookcases. It was an eerie place, one more haunting than inviting, and Michael felt an illogical fear setting in. There were more floors to explore, but he knew he would never reach them because the dream always ended before he had a chance to ascend to the next level. God only knew what was up there, *waiting for him*. Like always, he awoke with a gasp. Damn, but if it wasn't time to get up anyway.

****

That morning, Michael brought a Bloomingdale's shopping bag to work with him. At lunchtime, he closed his office door, unlocked his file drawer and transferred the $10,000 from his leather case to the shopping bag. Cautiously, he covered the cash with a copy of *The New York Times*, so no one would see what was inside. Then, package in hand, he discreetly emerged from his office. "I'll be back after one," he told his assistant Angela as he passed her cubicle in the hall.

"Returning something to Bloomie's?" she inquired, noticing the bag.

"Oh ... yeah. An exchange," he muttered, moving on without elaborating.

It was a short walk to the Plaza. Nevertheless, Michael was apprehensive and wary of his surroundings. Lunchtime workers and tourists flooded the streets, and traffic seemed more hectic and heavy than usual. Tense and jittery, he kept a firm grip on the shopping bag and held it in front of him rather than at his side, fearful that someone might snatch it. He arrived at the fountain across the street from the hotel entrance at precisely 12:30. Standing in plain view, he scanned the swarming crowd of loiterers and pedestrians. Recognizing no one, he sat down on the edge of the fountain and waited anxiously, his hand still tightly wrapped around the handle of the shopping bag tucked between his legs.

Typically, few people took notice of him. That was the ironic thing about life in New York – so many people going out of their way not to pay attention to one another. There was one notable exception – a mounted police officer, stone-faced in helmet and sunglasses, peering down at Michael from his horse as they sauntered along Central Park South. Michael couldn't help but stare back, wondering if the cop was psychic, following him with his guilty eyes until he faded from view and Michael could finally exhale. It was then and there that the reality of the situation became unnervingly clear: *I'm sitting outside the Plaza Hotel with $10,000 of my hard-earned savings in a shopping bag, intended for a man I hardly know who has agreed to kill my wife's murderer. Am I really going to go through with this?*

Lost in his reverie, Michael didn't notice when someone silently sat down beside him. He finally glanced to his left and flinched when he saw Butch's profile. "A little edgy, aren't we?" Butch murmured, looking straight ahead.

"You're late," said Michael, also avoiding eye contact.

"Sorry," Butch mimicked. "I was ... detained."

Tit for tat, Michael noted, realizing that he was dealing with a guy who always had to get even.

"I see you like to shop," Butch teased, referring to the shopping bag.

"It's all there," Michael assured him, anticipating the question. "$10,000 in cash."

"Good," said Butch. "Just walk away and leave it."

Michael turned his head and stared at him. "Just *leave it?*"

"Don't tell me you want a fucking receipt."

"No, but how about a little reassurance?"

Butch looked off, smiling and shaking his head. "Christ, you're really insecure. You know that?"

"Yeah, I'm funny that way," Michael remarked.

"You're afraid I'm going to take the cash and you'll never hear from me again, is that it?"

"Wouldn't you be?"

"No such luck, smiley," Butch assured him. "I'm in this for 20,000. Not 10. Besides, I have a reputation to uphold."

"Yeah," said Michael. "I'm sure customer service is your top priority."

"Hey, pal," Butch chuckled, lighting a cigarette. "*You* called me. Remember? Whoever gave you my number knew what he was doing."

Michael relented. "So what happens next?"

"Next, I pay your friend Wendt a little visit and put him out of your misery. If that's okay with you."

"Just like that?"

Butch took a deep drag. "Just like that," he exhaled slowly, smoke streaming from his lips and nostrils. "I already checked things out. Schedules, logistics, et cetera. Everything should go like clockwork. Yeah, after tomorrow night, all your troubles will be over."

Michael straightened up. "You're doing it *tomorrow* night?"

"You got a problem with that?"

"No. I ...I just didn't expect it to be so soon."

"The sooner it's done, the sooner I get the rest of my money," Butch reasoned. "Also, the sooner you can put all this unpleasantness behind you. Right?"

Michael didn't answer. Instead, he gazed at a row of hansom carriages lined up at the curb by the park. He recalled the time he took Karen for a ride, but didn't remember whether the occasion was Valentine's Day, her birthday or their anniversary. It was something they had always talked about doing, and one of the few things on Karen's wish list Michael had made good on. Yet all they joked about afterwards was the pungent smell of horse manure that had permeated the event.

"Tomorrow's Friday," Butch noted. "Leave town after work," he instructed. "Establish your alibi like I told you. I'll call you when it's over. I'll leave a message on your answering machine, a wrong number from someone looking for Manny. That's how you'll know it's been done. Or, if you prefer, check the papers on Sunday … I'd look in the *Daily News.*"

But Michael wasn't really paying attention. He had suddenly felt a wave of nausea rising from the pit of his stomach. "You know ..." he said falteringly. "Maybe we're being a little hasty here."

Butch glanced at him and smirked. "What? Are you kidding me?"

"I mean, what's the rush? Maybe we need to … to think about this a little more."

"There's nothing to think about," said Butch, toking on his smoke. "We're beyond the thinking stage. It's time to act. Time to put the plan into action."

"I don't know," Michael fretted. "I don't know if I can …"

"He didn't just kill your wife," Butch firmly and bluntly pointed out, flicking his ashes. "He *butchered* her – slit her belly, slashed her hands, her face ... her throat. He left her bleeding on the pavement ... like he was putting out the trash."

Michael shuddered. He didn't need to be reminded of just how heinous a crime Leon Wendt had committed. He vividly recalled the night that Karen didn't come home, his frantic calls to her office, her sister and her friends. He remembered the exact time – 1:11 a.m. – when the police came knocking on his door. He recalled the long trip downtown to the morgue to identify Karen's body, the anesthetic smell of the bleak corridors, the flickering fluorescent ceiling lights, the indifference of the staff, and the deep, gaping lacerations on Karen's naked body …

"*You owe it to her*," Butch added for good measure, dropping his cigarette on the pavement and crushing it with his heel. "… if not to yourself."

"Well …" said Michael wistfully. "You've obviously done your homework."

"Just leave the bag," Butch replied. "I'll take care of the rest."

Swallowing hard, Michael relaxed his grip on the shopping bag handle. Then he rose unsteadily to his feet and began to walk away, drifting effortlessly into the cross-current of strangers coming and going. Of course, he paused to look back. But by then, both Butch and the shopping bag were gone. Michael felt a sudden raindrop or two tapping him on the shoulder. *What's done is done*, he thought, moving on.

IX
_____

It wasn't supposed to be like this. He was supposed to feel
relieved, exuberant, avenged – anything but anxious, indecisive
or guilty. Yet Michael was plagued with these conflicting emotions
from the moment he sealed the deal with Butch. It was one thing
to grieve, to feel anger and bitterness, but another to allow his
pain to lead him down this particular road. The last thing Michael
had expected was second thoughts.

But there they were, clear as day, gnawing at him, forcing him
to face the reality of whom he was and what he was becoming.
Oddly, it wasn't the threat of incarceration that troubled him – it
was the indelible stain of another man's blood on his hands.

Michael was so preoccupied with these thoughts that he forgot
it was a casual Friday at Paragon Books. Realizing his oversight
as soon as he arrived, he removed his jacket and tie and loosened
the top button of his starched white shirt. But he still felt out of
place and out of touch. Much of the senior staff had taken the day
off for a long weekend in their havens of choice. Yet it was anything
but a quiet day for Michael.

There were galleys to proof, schedules to adjust, and revisions
that had to be discussed with a notoriously difficult author. And
also, there was the unexpected visit from Lieutenant Philip Navarro
of the NYPD. "Good afternoon, Mr. Gray," he declared, suddenly
standing in Michael's doorway. "I hope I'm not intruding."

Oh, my God, thought Michael. *It was a set-up. Butch was an* *undercover cop. I gave him $10,000 to kill somebody. Conspiracy to commit murder. Ten to 20 years in prison. Why else would the detective assigned to Karen's case show up here after all these months?*

But Lt. Navarro's tentative manner suggested otherwise. He was actually waiting for permission to enter the room. It soon became obvious that he wasn't there to bust anyone. As the initial shock began to wear off, Michael composed himself and rose from his chair. "No, not at all. Please, come in," he said, reaching out to shake the lieutenant's hand. "Have a seat."

Slightly overweight and considerably world-weary, Navarro slumped into the leather chair beside Michael's desk and rendered a sigh. "I know it's been awhile since I last spoke with you," he admitted, primly folding his hands on his lap, "but I just thought I owed you a visit."

Michael glanced at Karen's portrait on the desktop, then looked into Navarro's baleful brown eyes. "You don't owe me anything, Lieutenant," he replied.

"Not even an apology? I can't imagine how hurt and disappointed you were that Leon Wendt was acquitted."

"No," Michael agreed. "You can't. But then, I can't blame you for that," he conceded. "I know you tried your best to get a conviction. I guess you just tried a little too hard."

Navarro ran his stubby fingers over his dark but graying goatee, a habit that often preceded an instance of wishful thinking. "You know, there's always the chance that Wendt will slip up and ..."

"And kill someone else?" Michael interjected. "Yeah, maybe we'll get lucky and that will happen. Then we can go through a whole new trial ... when the court gets around to it."

Navarro let the remark slide. He was all too aware of Michael's pain and frustration. It was understandable – and common. Besides, after 13 years in Homicide, he was just as outraged, if not as cynical. Still, he felt obliged to offer Michael some modicum of hope. "I know that sometimes it seems as if there's no justice in this world," he said. "But there is."

Michael merely humored him with a knowing smile.

"I've seen a lot of killers walk, Mr. Gray," said Navarro. "But

I've never seen one who got *away with it*. Call it karma or …
whatever. But what goes around comes around. Some of these
career criminals can't resist stepping out of line. Consequently,
they sometimes end up on the wrong end of a gun. Some just get
careless and step in front of a bus. Some drink themselves to death
or overdose on bad crack. And some …"

Michael listened but Navarro didn't complete his sentence.
Instead, he opted for the heart of the matter. "The hardest thing is
letting go," he admitted. "But you have to – or else it eats you up
inside."

"Who are we talking about here, Lieutenant?" asked Michael
with a curious gaze. "You or me?"

Navarro lowered his head and smiled sadly. "Okay, I probably
have had as many sleepless nights as you."

"Oh, I doubt that, lieutenant," said Michael, biting his lip. "Like
they used to say, there are eight million stories in the Naked City.
And mine … is just one of them."

Navarro shifted uneasily in his chair. "I just wanted you to
know that you're not forgotten – that I haven't given up."

Michael didn't know how to respond appropriately to that.
The irony of the situation was beyond his comprehension. In a
matter of hours, Leon Wendt would be dead and here, prophesizing
his eventual doom, was the man who arrested him. Imagine
Navarro's surprise when he hears of Wendt's rendezvous with
karma. Michael didn't know whether to laugh or cry. All he knew
was that his heart was beating so fast that he feared it would
explode. Internal panic was starting to set in and it wouldn't be
long until he started to hyperventilate. "Well," he finally said
breathlessly. "Thank you, Lieutenant. I sincerely appreciate your
kindness. It was considerate of you to remember me."

Fortunately, Navarro had run out of things to say. Awkwardly,
he rose to his feet and lumbered toward the door.

Pressing his luck, Michael nonetheless felt compelled to add,
"Let me know if anything happens."

Navarro paused and looked at him quizzically.

"I mean … if there are any new developments in the case,"
Michael clarified.

Navarro nodded, then turned and left.

Michael took a deep breath, then another. His brow had broken out into a cold sweat, and he suddenly realized that his hands were trembling. He saw things with a new clarity and he was more than ill at ease. He was convinced that he had made the biggest mistake of his life. But, thank God, there was still time to rectify it.

X

_____

Michael was on pins and needles, pacing his living room floor, waiting for Butch's call. When the phone finally rang, he fairly jumped out of his skin. "Hello?" he huffed into the receiver.

"You beeped me," said Butch.

"Yeah. Look," said Michael anxiously. "I've been doing a lot of thinking …"

"Oh? About what?"

"About our arrangement," Michael replied. He hesitated, then summoned the nerve to declare, "I want to cancel it."

The silence on the other end of the line was deafening. "Sorry," Butch finally intoned. "No can do."

"Wh-wh-what do you mean?" Michael stammered.

"Once I start a job, I always see it through."

"No, you don't understand," said Michael with a nervous laugh. "I've reconsidered."

There was no reply.

"You can keep the $10,000 deposit," Michael hastened to add. "I don't care about that. Just don't carry out the contract."

"I'm afraid you're the one who doesn't understand," Butch sternly replied. "You and I made a *deal* – I take care of the guy who did your wife and you pay me $20,000."

"Yes, but I've changed my mind."

"Oh, really?" said Butch, his voice oozing sarcasm. "Well, I'm afraid it's a little late for that, Mr. Gray. As a matter of fact, I'm on my way to take care of it right now. Christ! We shouldn't even be talking about this over the goddamn phone! If you've got cold feet, I suggest you go some place nice and warm. If you catch my drift ..."

Michael couldn't believe his ears. The man had $10,000 of his money and was under no obligation to fulfill the contract. What more did he want? "Perhaps I'm not making myself clear ..."

Suddenly, there was an abrupt click. "Hello? Hello?" said Michael, standing in the middle of his kitchen with the telephone receiver pressed to his ear. *He hung up*, he realized incredulously.

Michael scrambled to search for Butch's beeper number, but before he could redial, his phone rang again.

"Listen to me," said Butch, his voice controlled yet seething with quiet anger. "Listen *very carefully*. I don't play games. I don't have the patience for it. My time and my services are valuable. You can't tell me one minute you want somebody dead and then turn around and say, 'Oh! I've changed my mind.' It doesn't work like that, smiley. Do you understand? *We are past the point of no return*."

"But ..." Michael tried to interject.

"Don't give me any of your fuckin' lip!" Butch snapped with a viciousness that sent a chill through Michael. Just as quickly, his tone became coldly subdued. "We had a deal," he firmly reiterated. "And I intend to see this job through. End of conversation. And don't do anything stupid – like trying to prevent it – because you'll only get yourself implicated and then you'll put me in jeopardy, too. Believe me, you don't want to do that. You do and I'll have no choice but to come looking for *you*. Do I make *myself* clear?"

"Why are you doing this?" asked Michael, bewildered. "You can walk away with $10,000 – for doing *nothing*."

"A deal's a deal," Butch stubbornly insisted. "Now just shut up, hang up the phone and go establish an alibi. I'll call you when it's over. Goodbye."

"No, wait!" Michael pleaded. But Butch had already hung up. "Shit!" he hissed, slamming down the receiver.

God, Michael shuddered. *What am I going to do now?* He folded his arms and doubled over with intense trepidation. This was all wrong, but how could he avert it if the man wouldn't listen to reason? He considered calling Lieutenant Navarro and leveling with him. Maybe he would understand what drove him to do such a foolish thing. *No, no – what am I, crazy?* The police could not be involved. Only he could stop this. But how?

Michael checked his wristwatch. It was 8:15 p.m. His mind was racing. Wendt lived cross-town and north. He had an unlisted number. It would take at least 20 minutes to get to his apartment. Depending on where Butch had called from, perhaps Michael would have enough time to get to him first. Wasting no time, he grabbed his raincoat and ran out the door.

Naturally, the elevator was making local stops on all the lower floors, so instead Michael took the stairs, stumbling twice as he rushed around the winding landings. When he reached the lobby, he paused in the doorway before proceeding, then strolled calmly but briskly to the nearest exit so as not to call attention to himself or arouse suspicion.

Out on the street, he started to hail a cab, then thought better of the idea. A taxi could cut through the park and get him where he was going faster, but cabbies keep records of their pickups and destinations. Something warned him to be as inconspicuous as possible. *No reason to panic*, he rationalized, *I've got enough time.* So he opted for a cross-town bus and an uptown train, wondering along the way how he would deal with the situation when he got there. Confront Butch or warn Wendt? This was crazy, dangerous. But the alternative – doing nothing – would be worse. It would haunt him for the rest of his days.

Of course, things never turn out quite the way one imagines or hopes they will. Deep down inside, Michael knew this all too well. Sure enough, when he emerged from the subway and turned the corner a half a block from Leon Wendt's address, he was stopped in his tracks by the sight of revolving red lights. No less than three police cars were double-parked outside of Wendt's building. A small throng congregated on either side of the entrance and were kept at bay by two uniformed officers. Against his better judgment, Michael cautiously advanced toward the scene, but paused and remained toward the back of the crowd.

"What's going on?" he discreetly asked a young black man in a New York Yankees windbreaker.

"I don't know," he replied, barely glancing in Michael's direction. "Some guy got shot or something."

Michael shuddered. *Got shot?* Was it Wendt? What was his condition? Was he alive or dead? Had anyone seen Butch? Could he have been caught in the act, confessing everything to the police at this very moment? Was it foolish to be here at the scene of the crime? Of course, but Michael couldn't leave. He needed to know exactly what had happened.

Then he thought he overheard a Hispanic woman say, "6K." Michael moved closer to where she was standing and talking with another woman. "Something wasn't right with that guy ..." he distinctly heard her say.

"I understand he had a criminal record," the other, older woman rather loudly revealed.

"He was up on a murder charge a year or two ago."

"Get out of here ..." her friend gasped.

"Mm-hm. He got off."

"Oh, my God. And he was a neighbor of ours?"

"Not anymore, he ain't."

It had to be Wendt they were talking about. But if it was, was he really dead?

There was no trace of an ambulance – just the squad cars. Not a good sign. Still, Michael lingered in the suddenly chilling breeze, hoping to learn more. He waited and waited. Then, when a van from the coroner's office arrived, it was obvious that the only way Wendt would leave the building was in a body bag. Stunned, Michael stood and watched as two attendants entered the building, then slowly drifted away from the morbidly curious crowd and began walking in the opposite direction.

A profound sense of guilt accompanied him as he trekked eastward on 111th Street and then southward along Central Park West, his head bowed and his hands buried in his raincoat pockets. As he wandered from block to block, recklessly navigating the flow of opposing pedestrian traffic, he reflected on the events of the last several days.

What had been accomplished by hiring Butch to kill Wendt? Karen was still dead and the grief of her brutal murder still gnawed at his heart. Only now there was fresh blood on his hands and another thorn in his conscience. If this was justice, it had a bitter taste, one so rancid that it made him sick to his stomach. He had badly misjudged his own resolve. There was no such thing as closure – only the pain of shame and fear to replace the pain of anger and loss.

Instead of taking the cross-town bus, Michael decided to continue on foot, trudging thirty-nine blocks and entering Central Park at 72nd Street. At that hour, some would think better of the idea, but he didn't care. He knew he would probably find his way home unscathed. And if he didn't, so be it. Perhaps he deserved a good mugging – or worse.

As it turned out, there was something strangely consoling about the park at night. Though surrounded on all sides by the towering monoliths of Manhattan, it was a dark and peaceful refuge that offered sanctuary from the glaring reality of the city it served. Following a winding path that seemed to stretch on forever, Michael pondered the past, present and future.

It was a familiar trail, one he had tread several times with Karen in the light of day. He recalled how they had strolled, arm in arm, in the midst of autumn, talking incessantly, plotting their futures. Occasionally, they strayed across an open meadow, circumvented a serpentine lake, scaled boulders the size of languid elephants, as if on an expedition through an uncharted land. The world was theirs, and their world was wide open.

Holding back the tears, Michael realized that Karen had been everything to him – wife, lover, confidante and friend. But now she was gone, and he believed it was as much his fault as her killer's. Wendt was dead and it was as much his fault as it was Butch's. Now, what would he do, assuming he could live with himself? Confess the whole sorry mess to the police? Throw himself on the mercy of the court? What would that accomplish except guaranteed prison time? Butch was nothing more than a beeper number – he would probably escape prosecution, easily folding his tent and disappearing in a puff of smoke. Even if he didn't turn himself in, Michael could become a murder suspect. It had been foolish of him to think he could stop this runaway train, even more foolish to have gone to the scene of the crime — someone might have seen him there. Someone could identify him. He should have established that alibi. He should have ...

The gun.

Michael abruptly stopped walking. What if the police were to search his apartment and find the Beretta? He could tell them he had bought it for his own protection after Karen's death. But that wasn't true. He bought it after Wendt was acquitted and there was documentation to prove it. Okay, okay, but what are the chances that the gun used to kill Wendt was of the same caliber? Slim, at best. Nevertheless, Michael wasn't taking any chances. He started walking again, then broke into a sprint, racing to the park exit at Fifth Avenue.

When he finally reached the door of his apartment, Michael fumbled with his keys. "Come on!" he demanded, poking desperately at the lock, until he finally managed to insert and turn the appropriate key. Once inside he hurried to the wardrobe closet in his bedroom. Tucked in a corner, behind a stack of empty shoe boxes, he found the wooden, velvet-lined case containing the Beretta. Thinking fast, he snatched the box and brought it to the kitchen. There, he removed the gun, placed it in a large food storage bag and stashed it in the freezer beneath a pile of frozen steaks. He then discreetly stepped out of his apartment into the abandoned hallway and disposed of the case down the nearest incinerator chute.

When he returned to his apartment, Michael noticed that the light was flashing on his telephone answering machine. At first, he refused to acknowledge it. But curiosity overpowered his dread. His heart pounded as he reticently approached the device and pressed the play button. "Yeah, hi," said a voice that Michael recognized as Butch's. "This call is for *Manny*. Your car is ready."

Michael shivered and hastily erased the message. Then he rummaged through the closet in the hall, searching for an opened Christmas gift. When he found the bottle of Chivas Regal, he peeled off the label and poured himself a glass. He winced as the first gulp of warm Scotch scorched his throat. *Oh, God,* he thought, running his hand through his hair. *Just let me get through this. Let this be the end of it. Please.* Yet something told him that this nightmare of his own making was far from over. What Michael didn't know was that, in fact, it had only just begun.

XI

An hour after he had murdered Leon Wendt, Butch arrived at his Edgewater, New Jersey home. No sooner had he crossed the threshold of his modest, two-bedroom, single-family house than he received a warm, wet welcome from Jet. The sleek, black Doberman pinscher affectionately licked her master's hand and submissively rolled onto her back, whimpering a plea for his caress. Butch obliged, crouching to stroke the canine's velvety chest and issuing words of doting endearment.

Then, rising slowly, he glanced at his answering machine on a nearby credenza in the hall. The good news was that there were no messages. The bad news was that there were no messages. Shrugging off his chagrin, Butch removed his leather jacket and tossed it onto the living room couch. He ran his hands through his wavy gray hair, moaning wearily. All he wanted to do was take a hot bath and get to bed, but first he needed a late night snack.

As he spread a generous helping of spicy brown mustard on his Dagwood sandwich, Butch marveled at the sheer artistry of his evening's handiwork – how deftly he had slipped into Wendt's building undetected and climbed stealthily to the sixth floor, how he used fake police identification to gain access to Wendt's apartment, then smoothly drew his gun and ordered Wendt to move inside. The stupid bastard thought he was being robbed. With the barrel of the weapon to his temple, Wendt calmly encouraged Butch to take his stereo (his two-bit, three-CD, Taiwanese "music system," for Christ's sake!) and cheap, gold-plated jewelry – never wondering why the gun was equipped with a silencer or why Butch was wearing a surgical glove, never expecting him to pull the trigger. Imagine his fleeting surprise as the weapon discharged and a .38 caliber bullet tore through his skull, splattering bits of his brain on a nearby lampshade.

It took a few seconds for his legs to go out from under him and his body to crumble to the floor. The look on his face – eyes glazed, mouth gaping – was priceless. Then it was just a matter of unscrewing the silencer, pressing the gun against Wendt's lifeless hand for palm and fingerprints, and leaving the unregistered weapon within inches of the body. In a matter of seconds, Butch emerged unnoticed from the apartment and left the building as discreetly as he had come.

The sweet memory made Butch chuckle with glee before he sank his teeth into the delectable sandwich. "Mmmm," he raved, savoring his creation. Jet regarded him with a quizzical stare. "Mmmm," he repeated with his mouth full, arousing Jet to fretful envy. "Mmmmmm!" he moaned emphatically until he coaxed Jet's drooling tongue and a bark of frustration from her gaping jaws. Butch loved to taunt his pet, to remind the bitch who was the boss. Although that was as far as his sadistic streak went with his one true friend. Alas, people were another matter.

Growing up alternately in Hell's Kitchen on the west side of midtown Manhattan and the Sheepshead Bay section of Brooklyn, Butch learned the power of intimidation early in life. The wayward son of an enforcer for a prominent underworld figure, he spent as much of his childhood roaming the streets of all five boroughs as he did sustaining the brutal discipline of a parochial education at the hands of Dominican nuns and Christian Brothers. In the schoolyard, he was a merciless bully, coercing cowering honor students out of their lunch money, indulging a penchant for sadistic acts against stray animals, and beating the piss out of anyone who challenged his authority. During the ages of ten through twelve, he explored the darker regions of the metropolitan area with a pack of Italian- and Irish-American friends sharing one common objective – to get into as much trouble as possible. A day's fun would include rolling drunks in Pennsylvania Station, verbally abusing the cheap whores in the vicinity of the Lincoln Tunnel, shoplifting adult books and copies of *Playboy* from cigar shops and magazine stands along Ninth and Tenth Avenues, and riding subway cars from Coney Island to Washington Heights and back. It was during this period that Butch took up smoking, spitting, cursing and pitching pennies – not to mention running numbers for his uncle and learning the many practical uses of a switchblade knife.

At thirteen, he lost his virginity – literally and figuratively. The former involved a family wedding reception, his eighteen-year old second cousin Louise, and the back seat of his father's Pontiac. The latter involved serving as the lookout for a warehouse break-in that netted approximately $70,000 worth of electronic equipment. By eighteen, Butch was taking a more active role in a series of burglaries, hijackings and fencing operations for his father's employer. It was only when his old man was found with three bullets in the back of his head in the trunk of a sedan in the New Jersey marshlands that Butch decided it was time to move up in the world.

At the age of nineteen, Butch ceremoniously began his career as a professional contract killer. His first target was a state's witness in a racketeering trial. Using his acquired skills as a second-story man, Butch managed to elude a pair of donut-gorging plain clothes cops parked outside in an unmarked vehicle, and gained entry to the witness's house through a basement window. Silently, he made his way upstairs and found the guy dozing in an easy chair in front of his big-screen TV. While Johnny Carson traded barbs with Don Rickles, Butch pressed the barrel of his gun against the back of the heavily padded headrest and pulled the trigger. The muffled shot had the desired effect – one fatal bullet lodged in the brain, no exit wound. Amused by the onscreen banter, Butch pulled up a chair next to his victim and watched the show until the commercial break, then departed the way he came – like a thief in the night.

Suspecting nothing, the cops didn't find the body until the next morning. By then, Butch was on a flight to Las Vegas where he would parlay his fee into a small fortune at the crap tables. The defendant in the case, an upper-level *capo* for a prominent Brooklyn family, walked and didn't look back. Like a first love, Butch's first kill was a fond memory.

Having acquired a taste for blood, he continued in this lucrative line of work. For the next twelve years, his services were strictly under the auspices of his late father's employer who was in the process of expanding his business interests. It was during this era that Butch (short for butcher) earned his nickname after running the CFO of a meat packing company through his own industrial grinder. Despite his growing reputation as an effective hired gun, Butch wisely kept a low profile below the omnipresent radar of federal prosecutors. Consequently, when some rather incriminating wiretaps finally put his boss behind bars for the rest of his life, Butch emerged unscathed from the subsequent investigations. In fact, his fortunes multiplied as he was now free to pursue a career as a free lancer, rather than as a devoted family man.

In his prime, Butch pulled down more money per year than the President of the United States. Of course, it was a time of mergers, acquisitions, hostile takeovers and reorganization. The old had to make way for the new, and a lot of bad blood had to be purged from the system. Somewhere along the line, Butch lost count of how many men (and a few women) he had killed over the years, but he estimated it was more than fifty and less than a hundred.

As a confirmed bachelor, Butch steered clear of steady girlfriends, most of whom he considered nothing more than manipulative gold diggers. He preferred the company of high-priced call girls and escorts who expected nothing but a payoff from him. "Love 'em and leave 'em a C-note – " that was his philosophy. It certainly beat alimony payments, and was one less millstone around the neck of a guy who liked to travel light. A wife wouldn't only cramp his style and limit his options, but could also put a strain on his precious nest egg. There were no such things as 60-year-old hitmen, he kept reminding himself. He had to save for his retirement while supporting the extravagant lifestyle he had grown accustomed to.

Yet by the time Butch reached forty, demand for his services began to decline. Most of his clientele was either dead, incarcerated, under surveillance or in the Federal Witness

Protection program. They were summarily replaced by a new crop of professionals – refugees from Third World countries who neither trusted nor respected craftsmen of the Old School.

Butch sorely missed those big paydays when a major hit would fetch upwards of fifty, seventy-five, even one hundred grand. Nowadays, the contracts were far and few between, while a string of bad investments during the technology bubble and careless gambling had chipped away at most of his nest egg. No sooner would he make a little cash than he'd have to turn it over. In fact, he had already handed over Michael Gray's $10,000 deposit to his bookie, a mere dent in his overall debt. The idea of parting with the remaining $10,000 was too painful for Butch to contemplate. Perhaps he could take the money to the racetrack and run it up a bit, maybe sock away a few thousand. His recent run of bad luck had to change sometime. Once he was back on his feet financially, he could clean up his act, start playing the market instead of the ponies. All Butch needed was a personal computer, five or ten grand, and a few hot stock tips and he could retire in the Caymans at the age of forty-four and live the rest of his life like a king.

But first, Butch needed to pay his latest client a call. Just to be safe, he would wait a few days to make sure that Leon Wendt's death was ruled a suicide. It would also give Michael Gray a chance to reflect on the significance of his actions. Butch had been taken aback by Gray's anxious, last-minute call earlier in the evening. But that was just a knee-jerk reaction, typical of one of those guilt-ridden, Yuppie assholes. Plenty of Butch's previous clients had come down with a bad case of cold feet at the moment of truth, only to breathe a sigh of relief once the deed was done and their "problem" solved.

Gray was no different – just another spineless prick with an obsession for revenge, but without the intestinal fortitude to do it himself. Once he realized that Butch had done him an enormous favor, Gray would show him the appreciation he so richly deserved. But whether he did or not, there was still the matter of an additional $10,000. After all, a deal was a deal.

His hunger sated and feeling rather chipper, Butch poured himself some bourbon on ice. As he sipped his drink, he parted the Venetian blinds and peered out his living room window at the glittering skyline of Manhattan across the Hudson River. *So close yet so distant*, he thought. One day, it would be a vague memory. He would call it a career, put it all behind him and spend the remainder of his life basking in the sun and sucking pina coladas through a straw on some remote, tropical beach. There would be a great white house overlooking a scenic cove, a sleek 60-foot yacht docked in a nearby marina, a different hot-blooded senorita in his bed every night. All he needed was one big score, one good longshot, one hot IPO – one lucky break.

"Jet," Butch commanded, snapping out of his reverie. He heard the approaching patter of his pet's paws and turned on his heels. "Come, girl," he said, leading the way to the basement door.

Downstairs, Butch yanked a cord and switched on a naked lightbulb suspended from the ceiling. Before him hung a heavily padded, man-sized dummy that he often used to practice his kick boxing. He glanced down at Jet, who was poised at his side and panting with anticipation. Butch smiled and took a sip of his bourbon. Suddenly, he shouted, "Attack!"

Like a bullet, the Doberman sprang forward and sank her fangs into the dummy's thigh. Butch watched with imperious delight as his predatory canine growled fiercely and viciously thrashed her head from side to side, jiggling the helpless mannequin.

"That's it, girl! Kill! Kill! Kill!" he gleefully incited. Responding to his incessant commands, Jet gnawed on the dangling leg, then feasted voraciously on the dummy's neck and torso, leaping and yelping and snapping her jaws in a veritable frenzy.

"Good girl! Good girl!" Butch commended between gulps of his bourbon. "Kill that fucker! Rip him apart!"

Jet was relentless, mercilessly ravaging her prey until Butch decided that she and he had had enough for one night. "Heel!" he abruptly commanded.

The wild beast instantly complied, obediently crouching before her master.

Pleased, Butch turned to a nearby aluminum shelf, reached into a bag of dog biscuits and tossed Jet a reward. "Yeah … that's my baby," he purred into his glass and downed the rest of his drink.

XII

Michael hardly slept that night. But instead of tossing and turning in his bed, he sat in the living room, remote in hand, channel surfing from one end of the dial to the other. Except for a handful of gratuitously violent B-movies back-to-back on HBO, every other station ran an infomercial or a confrontational talk show, running the gamut of bogus emotions from amazed to irrationally exuberant to downright belligerent. Not that Michael was paying any attention or particularly cared. There was a tight knot in his stomach and a throbbing ache in the back of his head that all the mindless images in the world couldn't quell. It wasn't until 6:35 a.m. that he finally dozed off in his chair, dreaming of a vertiginous descent down spiral staircases into dark dungeons with voracious demons in hot pursuit.

Suddenly, the doorbell rang and Michael was jarred awake. The clock on his VCR read 10:45. Blaring Japanese anime cartoons were assaulting his senses. He fumbled with the remote until he managed to turn off the television. Then he rose wearily from his chair and staggered to the front door. He didn't bother looking through the peephole – he had an intuitive hunch who was on the other side of the door. Instead, he tried to compose himself, running his hands through his disheveled hair and tucking his shirt into his trousers. Finally, he unlocked and opened the door. "Lieutenant Navarro," he acknowledged, feigning surprise.

The perceptive detective immediately noticed the rings under Michael's eyes and the stubble of his unshaven face, but didn't jump to any conclusions. He merely nodded, "Mr. Gray."

"What brings you here on a Saturday morning?" asked Michael. "A new development in the case?"

Navarro's eyes narrowed with a glint of irony. "You could say that. May I come in?"

"Please," said Michael, stepping aside.

Navarro crossed the threshold and glanced around the foyer as if already looking for clues.

"May I take your coat?" Michael asked politely, closing the door.

"That won't be necessary," Navarro responded, catching a faint whiff of alcohol in the air.

"Something to drink?"

"No, thank you."

"Are you sure? I've got some ..."

"Leon Wendt is dead," Navarro abruptly announced, making an about-face.

Michael cocked his head. "Excuse me?"

Navarro pursed his lips. "It appears that he committed suicide."

Michael knitted his eyebrows, expressing concern and disbelief. "How?"

"How?"

"How did he kill himself?"

"Self-inflicted gunshot wound ... to the head."

"Wow," said Michael. "That's a shock."

"I'm a bit surprised myself," Navarro admitted, turning away from Michael and sauntered slowly into the living room. "He didn't strike me as the guilt-ridden, suicidal type."

"Well ... I guess you never know about some people."

"I guess not," Navarro replied evenly over his shoulder. The detective casually scanned the room – a force of habit. He noted the obsessive-compulsive order of things. Nothing out of place. Carpeting, furniture and fixtures as clean as a whistle. Unusual for an unmarried man, especially a widower. Eventually, his wandering gaze fell upon Karen's sainted picture frames and there remained until Michael's voice intruded upon his reverie.

"Did he leave a note or something?"

"A note?" Navarro echoed, turning his attention to Michael once again.

"A suicide note."

"No. In fact, he didn't make *any* kind of preparation. You know, put his affairs in order."

Detecting a hint of scrutiny in Navarro's voice, Michael knew that playing dumb wouldn't fly. He scratched his head and let out a sigh. "Well, I'd be lying, Lieutenant, if I said I was sorry to hear it."

"That's certainly understandable," Navarro allowed. "After all, he did get away with murder, didn't he? Guess you could say, he got what he deserved."

"Well ... I wouldn't put it that way," said Michael, maintaining unflinching eye contact. "It wasn't the end I wanted to see for him, but I must say ... it does provide a sense of closure."

"Not exactly," Navarro replied. "It isn't as cut and dry as all that. There are some unanswered questions."

"Such as?"

"Such as why none of Wendt's neighbors heard a gunshot. Or why the gun was found in his right hand .... I know for a fact that he was left-handed."

"Hmm, that *is* odd," Michael conceded, feigning bewilderment. After a moment's pause, he nonchalantly added, "You don't suspect foul play, do you?"

Navarro assumed a blank expression. "Should I?" he wondered aloud.

Michael shrugged. "It would certainly be poetic justice."

"That it would," Navarro agreed. "It would also constitute homicide, requiring a full investigation."

"Well, if that were the case," said Michael, "I'm sure there would be any number of suspects."

Navarro's eyes narrowed. "Or at least a few."

Stone-faced, Michael firmly held Navarro's stare for the longest ten seconds imaginable.

"Ahh, but who cares?" the detective finally muttered. "The guy was a scumbag. Everybody knows that. Whatever the circumstances of his death – the world's a better place without him ... Right?"

"I wouldn't disagree with that," Michael replied, wondering whether Navarro really felt that indifferent or if he was toying with him.

The lieutenant bit his lip and nodded. "Well, I'd better be on my way," he said, drifting toward the door. Of course, he hesitated, unable to resist one obvious question. "I just need to ask, where were you last night at ten p.m.?"

"Ten o'clock?" Michael took several seconds to recollect. "I was right here ... at home."

"Alone?"

"Well, yes. I'm afraid I don't do much socializing these days, Lieutenant."

"Can anyone corroborate your whereabouts? Did you speak with anybody on the phone? Say hello to a neighbor in the hall?"

"No, not a soul," said Michael, ignoring the impulse to devise an alibi. That would be too convenient. That's what Navarro would expect. *Just play it cool*, Michael told himself. There was nothing to tie him to Leon Wendt's death, nothing that linked him besides motive. An apparent suicide – that's all it was. There was no solid evidence that suggested murder. Butch was a pro, too good to make mistakes, too cunning to get caught.

Apparently, the reverse psychology worked. Navarro completely dropped the subject and reached for the door knob. "I'm sorry if I disturbed you on your day off," he paused to apologize. "You look pretty tired."

"Insomnia," Michael explained. "You know how it is."

Navarro nodded. "Yeah. I know how it is. Well, maybe now you'll sleep a little better."

"I doubt it," said Michael, gazing straight into the lieutenant's eyes, yet looking far beyond him.

Navarro nodded. "Take care."

"Don't be a stranger," Michael replied, watching as the detective walked away before slowly closing and locking the door behind him.

XIII

Alan Davis was on the Staten Island ferry, en route to his Wall Street office, when he learned about Leon Wendt's death. He was reading the Monday morning edition of the *Daily News* and there it was, black and bold, in a one-column, three-paragraph story buried on page seventeen: **ACQUITTED SLAY SUSPECT FOUND DEAD**. "Son of a bitch," Alan murmured under his breath.

He could have easily missed the article. In fact, he wished he had. "*...an apparent suicide ...*" the paper reported. "*... a self-inflicted gunshot wound ...*" But Alan knew better. It was too convenient and unlikely a demise. Leon Wendt had met with foul play. And although it was not he who had pulled the trigger, Alan nonetheless felt just as culpable.

Ever since he had provided Michael with the beeper number that had been furnished to him by one of his "connected" clients, Alan regretted doing so. But in his heart of hearts, he had been convinced that Michael would never act on his compulsion. He had hoped that Michael would have thought things through, would have considered the consequences, and would have ultimately realized the senselessness of retribution. But apparently he hadn't, and now Alan had to live with it.

There were so many things to live with these days, Alan scarcely knew where it all went wrong. One moment he was top man on campus, consistently on the dean's list, president of the debate team, star athlete and voted "Most Likely To Succeed." The next minute he was just another overpaid, underachieving financial advisor with a checkered resume, dubious clientele and a private list of sins he chose to overlook. Back in his college days, he may not have been much to look out, certainly not as handsome as Michael, but he had an outgoing personality and a sense of self that attracted others, especially women, nonetheless. Nowadays, divorced, paunchy and gradually balding, he relied more than ever on his gift for gab and six-figure salary to spark any interest in the opposite sex. If experience had taught Alan anything, it was that women were intuitive, and they knew a loser when they saw one.

And yet he could boast working for a prestigious Wall Street firm, as long as the little voice in his head didn't remind him that he had previously been employed by a now defunct company whose senior management had been convicted of bilking investors out of millions of their mutual funds. He now managed the portfolios of dozens of high-profile clients – and a few who preferred to keep a low profile, as well as bank accounts in Switzerland and the Cayman Islands. It was nothing to be ashamed of, but neither was Alan particularly proud of his professional stature. It was certainly a far cry from the life he had envisioned for himself – the one in which he was happily married with children, a captain of industry, the kind of man they named hospitals and libraries and sports arenas after. Instead, he was the kind of man who scalped tickets, hustled cocktail waitresses, and acted as an intermediary between his best friend and a contract killer.

After reading the story twice, Alan folded the newspaper and placed it on the vacant seat beside him. He turned his head and looked out the window, studying the vast expanse of the Narrows, the distant Palisades and the approaching Manhattan skyline, his mind twisting and turning down dark alleyways that led nowhere.

Eventually, he reached into his vest for his cellular phone and pounded out the only other number besides his own that he knew by heart. Michael answered on the third ring. "It's me," said Alan.

"Oh, hi," Michael replied rather routinely. "I was just on my way out the door. What's up?"

"... I just read about it."

"Huh?"

"It was in this morning's *Daily News*," Alan discreetly disclosed. "That ... *thing* we had been discussing."

"Oh, yes," Michael acknowledged, his tone surprisingly subdued. "Well ... there's more to the story."

"You want to talk about it?"

"Now?"

"No, later. Wanna' meet for lunch?"

"Yeah, why don't we do that."

"The usual place?"

"Sure."

"How does 12:30 sound?"

"Could we make it one o'clock?"

"All right. I'll see you then," said Alan. He waited until Michael hung up, then pressed the off button and returned the phone to his vest pocket. Glancing to his right, Alan noticed a pale, aging woman in black staring at him. He stared back until she was forced to look away. Then he retrieved the newspaper and reread the article. He still couldn't believe it. What was even more unbelievable was that he wished Leon Wendt were still alive.

XIV

Cynthia noticed it – there was something different about Michael Gray. Yet, to her vexation, she couldn't quite put her finger on what it was. It wasn't anything superficial like new clothes or a haircut. The clues were in his eyes, the manner in which he spoke, and even in his pensive silences – a deep, dark secret, perhaps, or a cathartic experience so profound that it had altered his entire persona. Did the others sitting around the conference table sense it, as well? Or was she the only one attuned to his – for want of a better expression – vibe? Something was definitely affecting him. She could tell that he was preoccupied during the editorial meeting. He was doodling more than usual on his spiral notepad, his thoughts obviously miles away from the business at hand. Something was definitely weighing on his mind, distracting him. But what could it be? A new woman in his life?

Oh, stop it, Cynthia chided herself. She was behaving like a silly schoolgirl with a crush on her chemistry teacher. It was bad enough that she fantasized about Michael in bed at night, imagining the two of them suddenly discovering an undeniable attraction, ultimately entangled in the throes of passion. At this rate, she was one step away from a diet of chocolate bon-bons and romance novels. Leave it to her to be attracted to a despondent widower who barely knew she existed. There were roughly eight million people in New York, yet she couldn't seem to find one guy who wasn't married, gay, abusive or psychologically tortured. Naturally, the more aloof and disinterested Michael was toward her, the more Cynthia was drawn to him. Studying his face from across the room, she wondered what it would be like to caress his taut yet tender cheek, to run her long fingers through his dark wavy hair, to kiss his soft, pouting lips and press her lithe, supple body against his ...

Suddenly, as if sensing her stare, Michael turned his head. Their eyes locked. Only this time, Michael didn't look away. He gazed at her with an intensity that made Cynthia's heart palpitate, simultaneously frightening and arousing her. She held her gaze – and her breath – for as long as she could. Then she shyly looked away, hoping that she hadn't given him the satisfaction of seeing her blush.

When the meeting finally adjourned, Cynthia hastily gathered her legal pad and cup of coffee and made a clean getaway to her office. But as she was about to close the door, Michael suddenly appeared before her. "Oh!" she couldn't help but gasp.

"Sorry," he said with a curious smile. "I didn't mean to startle you."

"No, that's ... okay," she replied with a nervous laugh. "I just ... wasn't expecting ..."

"I was wondering about that rain check," Michael said directly, dispensing with the usual repartee.

Cynthia tried not to look surprised. "Rain check?"

"Yeah. You had suggested a drink after work."

"You mean ... tonight?"

"Or tomorrow," Michael shrugged. "Or whenever you're available."

Cynthia hesitated and bit her lip.

"What's wrong?" asked Michael.

"Well, I've got a gyn ... er ... a doctor's appointment tonight," Cynthia fretfully confessed.

"Okay. Then how about ..."

"And a yoga class on Tuesday and dinner plans with my parents on Wednesday," she reluctantly added.

"I see," Michael muttered, getting that faraway look in his eyes again. "Well, in that case ..."

Cynthia's hopes were plummeting. Resigned to the inevitable letdown, she took a deep breath and braced herself. But unexpectedly, Michael's eyes brightened. "Then I guess I'll just have to take you out to dinner next weekend," he blithely declared, adding with a dash of uncharacteristic whimsy, "That is, of course, unless you're busy washing your hair."

Cynthia couldn't believe her ears, which is why it took her several seconds to respond. "No. No, I'm not busy next week. Dinner would be great."

"How does Saturday night sound?"

Wonderful, she thought. "Fine," she replied.

"Good," said Michael. "I guess we'll ... ah ... work out the how, when and where later."

"I'll e-mail you my phone number and address," Cynthia promised.

Michael nodded, amused by the novelty of dating in a new millennium. "Well," he awkwardly replied., realizing that he had suddenly run out of things to say. "Catch you later."

After he left, Cynthia got another stiff cup of black coffee and treated herself to a reality check by plunging into her work. Nevertheless, she had Saturday night on her mind for the rest of the day. Indeed, there was something different about Michael Gray. And whatever it was, she liked it.

****

"Am I late or are you early?" asked Michael as he joined Alan at their usual booth in Pete's Tavern on East 18th Street.

"Both," his friend replied, glancing at his wristwatch.

"I couldn't get a cab, so I took the subway."

"Whatever," Alan muttered with a wave of his hand. "I don't have to get back to work too soon."

Since one of them was headquartered in midtown and the other worked way downtown, they often met for lunch at this convenient halfway point. Usually they had a few beers with burgers and enjoyed a few laughs before getting back to the grind, but today the mood was decidedly different. After the usual small talk, there was an uneasy moment of silence between them that Alan finally felt obliged to relieve. "I have a feeling we're gonna' need a lot of drinks," he quipped, but without a trace of a smile.

"Not me," Michael declared, sitting straight and taking in his surroundings. "The more sober, the better."

"Want to tell me about it?" asked Alan, getting right to the point.

"I thought you didn't want to know anything."

"I lied."

"I called the number you gave me," said Michael. "I met the guy. He seemed to check out fine."

"And?"

"And I gave him a deposit."

Alan propped his elbows on the table and folded his hands. "So ... you actually went through with it."

"Not exactly," said Michael, keeping his voice low.

"What do you mean, *not exactly*?"

"I called it off. I canceled the contract."

Alan was baffled. "So ... what happened? Are you telling me that ..." He paused and looked around to make sure no one could hear them. "... you-know-who shot himself?"

"No. It wasn't suicide."

"But you called it off."

Michael leaned forward across the table and stared grimly at his friend. "I tried to stop him, Alan," he said in a hush tone. "I really did. But he wouldn't listen to me. He killed him, anyway."

Alan felt a chill run up his spine. He gaped at Michael until his palpitating heart slowed down. "So now what?"

Michael leaned back in his chair and shrugged. "What's done is done. I'm just going to have to live with it."

"That makes two of us," Alan replied uneasily. "I thought ..."

Michael raised his eyebrows curiously.

"I thought you would have a change of heart," said Alan.

"I did," Michael insisted. "But the guy ... he just wouldn't take no for an answer."

Alan stroked his chin anxiously. "I never thought it would go this far."

"Neither did I. It just ... got out of hand."

"*Out of hand*? Michael ... for Christ's sake ..."

"Look, you needn't blame yourself. *I* was the one who took the initiative. It's nobody's fault but mine."

Alan begged to differ, but he didn't press the issue. "You said you gave this guy a deposit?"

"$10,000."

"What about the rest of the money?"

"What about it?"

"How much do you owe him?"

"I don't owe him anything," Michael declared. "I called it off."

"But he went through with it."

"Against my wishes."

"That doesn't matter," Alan scoffed. "The guy's gonna' want the rest of his money."

"Well, that's too damn bad," said Michael defiantly. "He's not getting it. He's lucky he got the ten grand."

"You're gonna' hold out on him?"

"I wouldn't call it holding out. I mean, it's not like I signed an ironclad contract."

"Are you out of your mind?" Alan gaped. "Do you have any idea who you're dealing with?"

"Yes, I think I do," Michael replied. "And frankly, I don't care. He'll have to be satisfied with what he's got."

"If it's a question of not having enough cash, I could lend you some," Alan offered.

"I have the cash," said Michael. "I'm just not paying him another cent of blood money. It's the principle of the thing."

"Be careful, Michael," Alan warned. "If you think things have already gotten out of hand, there's no telling what could happen next."

"Nothing's going to happen," Michael predicted, placing his napkin on his lap and referring to his menu. "We just have to put this whole thing behind us and go about our business."

"I wish it were that simple," said Alan apprehensively. Perturbed by Michael's cavalier attitude, he impulsively reached across the table and clutched his friend's wrist.

"Will you at least keep me in the loop?" he appealed.

"Now why would you want me to do that?" asked Michael. "Haven't I imposed upon you enough already?"

"Hey," said Alan. "In spite of what you said, *I'm* the one who got you into this. If necessary, I'll be the one to get you out."

"What are you going to do, Alan?" Michael smirked. "Find me another hitman?"

"That's not funny," Alan replied. Nevertheless, he couldn't resist cracking a sardonic smile.

Not so the man with the thick gray hair and a scar on his neck as he watched them from the relative obscurity of a bar adjacent to the dining room. Having decided that he had seen enough, he crushed out his cigarette, took one last gulp of his beer, and left a five-dollar bill on the counter.

****

Later that afternoon, while he was proofreading copy, Michael got a call from his assistant Angela. "There's a Manny on the line for you," she announced.

"Who?" Michael muttered in bewilderment, then froze. "Oh ... Oh, yes."

"Shall I put him through?" asked Angela.

Michael wasn't expecting a call so soon. But it was probably better to get it sooner rather than later. "Yes, please," he told Angela, taking a deep breath.

There was a click, followed by an eerie silence, then Butch's unnerving, mellifluous voice. "Mr. Gray?"

"Speaking," said Michael evenly.

"Well, how are you?"

"How do you think?"

"I don't know ... relieved? Satisfied? Grateful?"

"None of the above."

"Gee, that's too bad," Butch lamented mockingly. "I had hoped you would feel a whole lot better. Especially now that you-know-who is you-know-what." He paused, expecting a reply. When none was forthcoming, he inquired, "What's the matter? You don't sound happy to hear from me."

"The last time we spoke, you hung up on *me*," Michael pointedly reminded him.

"You were hysterical," Butch claimed.

"No, I wasn't. You just didn't want to hear what I had to say."

"Yeah, well ... that was then, and this is now. My work is done. There's no heat to speak of. So I guess it's time to pay the proverbial piper, Mr. Gray."

Michael swallowed hard. "I don't think so," he firmly replied.

There was another long pause. "Excuse me?"

"You heard me. You've got $10,000 of my money. That's more than enough. Enjoy it."

Butch was perplexed. "Huh? What are you telling me?"

"I'm telling you that I never want to hear from you again," Michael declared. "As far as I'm concerned, you don't exist. I never met you. You don't know me and I don't know you."

"Hey, wait a minute, you ungrateful bastard," sneered Butch. "If you think you can talk to me like that, you've got ..."

But Michael didn't wait. He slammed down the phone and finally exhaled. Then he picked up the receiver and rang Angela. "It's me," he said. "Do me a favor. Hold all my calls ... Thanks."

Michael took a moment to compose himself. Then, feeling oddly exhilarated, he went back to work. In spite of what he had told Alan, he knew it would take time to put it all behind him. But at least he wanted to forget, and that was an important first step.

XV

The rap sheet on Leon Wendt was longer than a roll of toilet paper. At least that was the joke around the precinct. Six arrests for aggravated assault, five counts of disorderly conduct, four cases of drug possession, three illegal weapons charges, two armed robberies and – as one of his arresting officers once chimed – a partridge in a pear tree. Make that one indictment for second-degree murder. Yet, despite this prolific record, there had been only three convictions and a total of five and a half years of incarceration over the course of two decades.

Lt. Navarro had the whole sorry history laid out on his desk like the loose pieces of an obscene jigsaw puzzle. He sifted through page after page, trying to formulate a more accurate profile of Wendt than the one he had originally constructed. This, he concluded, was the appalling legacy of a man capable of anything – anything except, perhaps, suicide.

"Still obsessing over that dirtbag?" Detective Eddie Ross remarked, peering over Navarro's shoulder and breathing down the back of his neck. "If I were you, I'd be doin' a jig on his grave."

Navarro had no witty retort. He simply ignored his colleague, who took a seat at his own desk to peruse the daily sports page. It wasn't that Navarro didn't share the sentiment. He had always hoped that Wendt would screw up big time and give him another chance to bust his ass – if not put a bullet in him. It was one thing to commit a heinous act and another to walk on a careless technicality, making New York's finest look like inept Keystone

Kops. Even so, nothing disturbed Navarro more than a crime scene that didn't quite add up.

Never mind the fact that Wendt, who was left-handed, allegedly popped himself in the right temple. Or that none of his neighbors had heard the shot. There were several equally puzzling clues, including the burnt TV dinner in Wendt's oven. The fumes set off a smoke detector in the apartment, and the alarm led to the discovery of the body just fifteen minutes after the estimated time of death. Was that intentional? If not, why would Wendt place a meal in the oven just before taking his life? Also, the door to the apartment was found unlocked. Who, besides Jerry Seinfeld, would do such a thing in New York City? And yet, there was no sign of forcible entry and forensics had yet to turn up so much as another person's dandruff.

There was also the question of Wendt's state of mind. He had pleaded not guilty to every one of the charges ever filed against him – even in the face of overwhelming evidence. He was as irresponsible and remorseless as they came. Loser that he was, Wendt was not the kind of sociopath who hated himself. In fact, he was very much a survivor. After years of addiction to everything from hash to speed to heroin, he died totally clean. Also, he had recently started a new job at a messenger service where, according to his parole officer, he was doing as well as could be expected. He had enough money to pay his bills and had something, if not everything, to live for.

Another detail was particularly vexing: Since his last prison term for armed robbery, Wendt had steered clear of firearms for fear of violating his parole. Possession would have landed him back in prison, and he knew it. Most likely, Wendt's weapon of choice would be a standard hunting knife with a serrated blade – like the one used to carve up Karen Gray.

Navarro didn't need to refer to the file to remember the Gray case in vivid detail. It had haunted and frustrated him for nearly two years. Karen Clayton Gray, age 28, was on her way home one night when she was allegedly confronted and murdered by a man later identified in a lineup as Leon Wendt. Gray, the human resources director for (of all things) a major life insurance company, had worked late at her office on Park Avenue South and was on her way home. At approximately 9:10 p.m., she emerged from the Lexington Avenue subway station at 68th Street, walked a few blocks north, then east along 71st Street. It was there that she encountered an unknown assailant and was forced into an adjacent alley. The apparent motive was robbery. Reacting either through panic or *chutzpah* or both, Gray began to cry loudly for help and resisted. It was a fatal miscalculation. Infuriated, the assailant slashed and stabbed her savagely – 27 times to be exact. When Gray finally succumbed to her killer's attack, he wrested the handbag from her grip and fled, hurtling past a single witness who spotted Gray's body and immediately called 911 on her cellphone. Despite the conscientious efforts of paramedics, Karen Gray was pronounced dead at the scene. Her handbag, minus her wallet, was found in the gutter two blocks away with no fingerprints except her own.

The savage and senseless brutality of Karen Gray's murder shocked even jaded New Yorkers who, thanks to statistics indicating a significant decline in the city's murder rate, had been lulled into a false sense of security. The *Post* and *Daily News* fueled public outrage with a series of hysterical headlines, while the Mayor's rival in an upcoming primary exploited the tragedy to his own advantage. There was pressure on the New York Police Department to bring the perpetrator of this horrendous act to justice swiftly.

The witness identified Leon Wendt, a convicted felon and junkie, from a set of mugshots and subsequently picked him out of a lineup. Although the murder weapon was never recovered, Karen Gray's credit cards were found hidden in Leon Wendt's apartment. At the time of his arrest, Wendt was unemployed yet feeding a costly heroin habit. After several hours of relentless interrogation, he finally confessed to the crime.

It was an airtight case – until the trial. When Wendt's court-appointed attorney discovered that a search warrant actually had been issued an hour *after* the police searched his client's apartment, he successfully moved to have the incriminating evidence ruled as inadmissible. Wendt also recanted his confession, testifying in court that he had been coerced into admitting his guilt on videotape after being interrogated for ten hours and threatened – off camera, of course – with bodily harm of the genital variety. The defense also did a skillful job of discrediting the arresting officers who, it turned out, had each been suspended at various times in their long careers for relatively minor infractions. The jury was even instructed to disregard the defense's questions about public pressure to expedite the arrest and prosecution of Karen Gray's killer posed in cross-examination of certain prosecution witnesses, which nevertheless planted seeds of doubt.

But the final blow to the state's case came when the single eyewitness, a 69-year old grandmother, took the stand. Unaccustomed to court procedure and somewhat hard of hearing, the easily intimidated woman came across as confused and tentative in her testimony and in her assertion that Leon Wendt had indeed been the man she saw fleeing from the scene of the crime. The fact that she reluctantly admitted to being a recovered kleptomaniac with a thirty-six year old record for shoplifting – unbeknownst to the prosecution – didn't help her credibility, either. It was just enough to tip the jury toward reasonable doubt.

Navarro, who had spearheaded the investigation, took the verdict hard. He was the one who had had the unpleasant task of breaking the news of Karen Gray's death to her husband, the one who initially assured him – despite his better judgment – that her killer would definitely be brought to justice and punished. Feeling personally responsible for the fiasco, Navarro spent many a night thereafter staring into his beer at a local watering hole.

And now, almost two years after Karen Gray's murder, Leon Wendt was dead, presumably by his own hand. But while this twist of fate was a cause for celebration in the precinct, it provided no sense of satisfaction for Lt. Navarro. Dead or alive, Leon Wendt still stuck in his craw. The system had failed Karen and Michael Gray, and there was no getting around that painful reality. Twelve years in Homicide had made Navarro relatively immune to the gruesome discoveries he made virtually every week, but some acts of inhumanity never ceased to astound, confound and sicken him, including this one. And there was nothing worse than an unsolved mystery.

Suppose Wendt's death *was* a homicide. Who, besides scores of outraged New Yorkers, would have wanted him dead? Michael Gray certainly must have. But Navarro, who considered himself an excellent judge of character, doubted that he had anything to do with it. With or without an alibi, with or without a compelling reason to exact revenge, Gray was nothing more than a distraught spouse, a helpless victim who would sooner torture himself with grief and misplaced guilt for his wife's death than harm anyone else. He just didn't have it in him. Perhaps it was a crime without a clear-cut motive. Perhaps Wendt was the victim of a home invasion, a robbery or drug deal gone bad. Now *that*, would be poetic justice.

Then suddenly, another possibility crossed Navarro's mind. At first, he dismissed it as a silly notion, the product of a desperately groping imagination. But it lingered, and soon its plausibility began to take root. Funny that he hadn't thought of it before, but what if ...

"Ha! I don't believe it," Ross guffawed, noisily rustling the pages of his newspaper.

"Believe what?" Navarro replied, glancing over his shoulder, distracted.

"Some rookie for the Red Sox pitches nine and a third innings of perfect ball, then walks three batters to load up the bases, *then* gives up a grand slam to lose the game."

"You're right," said Navarro. "Pretty unbelievable."

Ross shook his head, then turned the page. "Talk about your hard luck. I guess nothing's a sure thing."

"No," Navarro wistfully agreed, regarding, then closing the Wendt file. "I guess not."

XVI

It was Michael's first date in nine years – and it was awkwardly obvious. He had been competent enough in choosing a well-reviewed French restaurant near Gramercy Park and making a reservation sufficiently in advance. He was thoughtful enough in picking up Cynthia at her apartment and bringing her a small bouquet of flowers. He was chivalrous enough in opening doors for her and telling her how lovely she looked that night. But when it came to making dinner conversation, Michael was clearly at a loss for words.

"So ..." he sighed after they had placed their order.

"So ..." Cynthia mimicked with big-eyed wonder and her most charming smile.

"I don't suppose you want to talk about work."

"Anything but."

"Hm. That's what I thought."

"Relax, Michael," said Cynthia, cutting him plenty of slack. "It's just dinner."

"Oh, I'm ... relaxed," he insisted, straightening his tie for the umpteenth time.

"Really." He paused, then admitted with a laugh, "I'm also a bit terrified."

"Well, of course," Cynthia teased. "I'm *very* intimidating. All one hundred and fifteen pounds of me."

"Seriously," said Michael. "I'm back where I was as a gangly, goofy teenager. I don't know what to talk about."

"Tell me about yourself," Cynthia suggested, planting her elbow on the table and setting her chin on the palm of her hand.

"What do you want to know?"

"Well, everything. But let's start with where you're from."

"Bridgeport, Connecticut," Michael replied. "Born and raised. And you?"

"Rockville Centre. That's out on the Island. *Long* Island."

"Yeah, I know where it is. I'm a well-traveled man."

"Do you have a family?" she asked. "Or were you raised by a pack of wolves?"

"Both, actually. My father was a lawyer. My mother was a school principal. When I wasn't being cross-examined, I was scolded and sent to detention." That provoked a smile from Cynthia, which heartened him. But then Michael's sly grin diminished as he added, "They divorced when I was in junior high."

"Any brothers or sisters?" asked Cynthia.

Michael shook his head. "I was an only child."

"That's too bad."

"Why? Did I miss out on something?"

"I have two brothers and two sisters," Cynthia revealed.

"That's a lot of sibling rivalry," quipped Michael.

"But a lot of emotional support."

"Comes in handy, does it?"

"At times," Cynthia conceded.

"Yes," said Michael, looking away momentarily. "I imagine it does."

"How did you end up in publishing? It's not a profession one sets his sights on as a child."

"I thought you didn't want to talk about work."

"We're not. We're talking about our career choices."

"I was a naive English Lit major," Michael admitted.

"Why naive?"

"I saw myself as the next great American writer."

"Didn't we all?" Cynthia scoffed.

"But I was exceedingly deluded," Michael insisted. "Melville, Hemingway, Updike, Gray ... I naturally assumed that the world was just waiting for me."

"Fiction?"

"What else?"

"I was going to write classic children's stories," Cynthia wistfully confessed.

"Wow, you were even more deluded than I was. Anyway, after several failed attempts, I became a copy editor at a now defunct history book publisher – just to pay the bills before I scored a bestseller and became a literary icon. A year later, I jumped ship to Paragon Books and .."

"... the rest is history," Cynthia interjected.

"Exactly."

They paused for a moment, then Cynthia chimed, "You see how easy it is?"

"What?" asked Michael.

"Talking to girls," she replied with a smile.

Indeed. There was something about Cynthia's smooth, playful style that helped put Michael at ease. He began to notice attractive little things about her – like the intriguing way the candlelight illuminated her flawless features, as well as the gracefulness of her elegant hands. There was also the scent of her perfume, different from Karen's fragrance but just as alluring. She noticed him staring at her and, rather than modestly looking away, savored his gaze with her own inquisitive eyes.

"Sorry," Michael apologized, sheepishly bowing his head.

Cynthia leaned forward and touched his hand. "I'm glad to be here with you," she simply and sincerely declared.

Michael looked up. The gesture comforted his conflicting emotions. "Me, too," he admitted.

After dinner, Michael and Cynthia took a long, leisurely walk uptown along Fifth Avenue, all the way to Rockefeller Center. It occurred to Michael that he had taken this walk before, quite a few times actually, with Karen, but he managed to suppress the memory. Mingling with tourists, they watched a handful of skaters glide on the milky white ice. Then they moved onward, strolling alongside Central Park en route to the Metropolitan Museum of Art. Along the way, they discussed all of the subjects that hadn't been covered over dinner – their favorite films, their guilty pleasures, their pet peeves, and their remarkably similar sociopolitical philosophies. Much to Michael's surprise, they had a great deal in common, and he would have been lying to himself if he didn't admit a definite attraction to Cynthia. Nevertheless, Michael resolved to keep it casual. He still wasn't ready to get involved with anyone and he didn't want to lead Cynthia on. He would simply walk her home, thank her for a lovely evening, refrain from the traditional goodnight kiss and return to the safe, uncomplicated solitude of his quiet apartment.

But when they reached the quaint, ivy-covered brownstone on 85th Street between Third and Second Avenues, Cynthia boldly took the initiative. "Come inside," she gently implored.

"Oh, I don't know ..." Michael hesitated. He glanced at his watch. "It's getting late and I've got ..."

Before Michael could finish his sentence, Cynthia grabbed him by the lapels of his raincoat and kissed him hard. Stunned, he held his breath, even after her soft, wet mouth slipped away. "Come inside," she repeated, taking him by the hand and leading him through the gate to her ground floor apartment.

When Michael finally exhaled, he was standing in Cynthia's living room, watching silently as she removed her coat and tossed it on the sofa. She then struck a match and lit several candles – one on a coffee table, two on a pair of end tables and another on the mantel of an artificial fireplace. Filled with a mixture of dread and anticipation, Michael waited patiently until Cynthia completed her ritual and returned to his side.

Face to face, they stared at each other like two leopards in a primordial forest. Both knew that instinct would inevitably win out, yet they hesitated, allowing the sexual tension between them to build to an unbearable peak. By then, it didn't matter who was the aggressor – both attacked with a startling passion. Their ravenous mouths devoured each other's. Their eager hands groped desperately, frantically removing and discarding each other's clothing until they were stripped completely bare. Careening and stumbling toward an adjacent room, they overturned a chair and knocked a poster off a wall along the way. Then they tumbled across the threshold and landed safely on the bed.

Entangled in each other's limbs, writhing in the rapture of a serpentine embrace, they decimated the barrier between them. For Michael, it was as if he were clinging desperately to life itself, marooned and adrift on a dark, uncharted sea. Could Cynthia be his island? *Rescue me*, he seemed to beg with each emphatic thrust.

****

It was practically dawn when Michael awoke, the room awash with intriguing shadows, the city outside beckoning with the sporadic flow of traffic. Quietly, he slipped out of bed and trudged to the bathroom. After washing his face, he gathered his clothes and dressed, trying to make as little noise as possible.

Cynthia stirred. "What time is it?" she asked.

"Go back to sleep," said Michael, sitting down on the edge of the bed and kissing her forehead.

"You're leaving?" she moaned.

"Yes. But I'll call you later."

"Will you?" she muttered, sounding doubtful.

"Of course," Michael gently laughed, stroking her hair reassuringly.

"Are you all right?" asked Cynthia.

"Mm-hm."

"Are you sure?"

In reply, Michael bent down and kissed her on the lips. "Now go back to sleep," he whispered. "I'll let myself out."

Savoring the cool morning air and the deserted city streets, Michael walked all the way home. It gave him time to reflect and to sort out his feelings. There were no regrets, no guilt to speak of. After all, he was an unmarried man. Although he still felt the sting of Karen's loss, still loved her and always would, he tentatively accepted the fact that she was gone while his own life went on. Wasn't he entitled to a little joy, a little pleasure in his otherwise lonely existence – especially after everything he had been through? Surely, Karen would have wanted it this way, would have wanted him to put aside his sorrow and enjoy a modicum of happiness. As for Cynthia, well ... it would be foolish to mistake one night of passion for love. But it was a promising start. All things considered, Michael felt pretty damn good.

One of the advantages of arriving home at 5:30 a.m. was that Michael didn't have to wait for the elevator. In less than a minute, he was sliding his key into the lock, quietly humming a Beatles tune and wondering how soon he should call Cynthia. He also considered sending her a gift – a dozen roses, perhaps. Yes, that would be a classy thing to do. There was hope for him yet.

As he entered his apartment, Michael flicked the light switch and closed and locked the door behind him. He tossed his keys into a bowl on a small buffet table, removed his raincoat and hung it in the alcove closet, then wandered wearily into the dimly lit living room. Collapsing on the sofa, he let out a loud yawn, tilted his head back and covered his eyes with the back of his hand. *What a night*, he thought. And what a strange, unpredictable world this was. One moment you could be at the end of your rope, and the next ...

Startled by a sudden creak, Michael lifted his head and opened his eyes. Staring back at him was Butch, pointing the barrel of a gun in his face. "Where's my money?" he solemnly intoned.

"How did you get in here?" Michael asked.

"Just answer my question. Where's ... my ... money?"

"What are you talking about?"

"Don't play games with me," Butch warned, pressing the gun to Michael's forehead.

"I'm not," Michael calmly assured him.

"So where's my money?"

"I don't owe you any money."

"Oh, no? No? $10,000. Does that ring a bell? We had a contract ..."

"The contract was canceled," said Michael, brushing the gun aside.

"The fuck it was!" snapped Butch, aiming between his eyes.

"I told you to back off," Michael said firmly. "You refused to listen. Now you expect me to *pay you*?"

"What is it about your present situation that you don't

understand?" Butch simmered, surprised at Michael's suddenly fearless attitude. Surely it was an act, or he was just plain crazy. "I have a gun pointed at your head. I will pull the trigger unless you pay me ... *now*."

"Well, that makes a lot of sense," said Michael sarcastically. "Kill me and you won't collect a penny."

"I don't care. This isn't only about money."

"Oh, no? Then what is it about, Butch? Control? Intimidation?"

"It's about honoring your commitments."

"Honor, my ass," Michael scoffed, rising to his feet. "You're a hitman. A career criminal. Who are you kidding? You have no 'honor.'"

Butch chortled in disbelief. "When did you suddenly grow a pair?"

"I don't know. Maybe it was when you hung up on me after I explicitly told you not to go through with it."

"A deal's a deal," Butch firmly maintained, keeping a bead on Michael as he moved slowly away from the sofa.

"For Christ's sake," Michael groaned in exasperation. *'We have no deal.'*

Butch cocked his revolver.

"Go ahead," dared Michael defiantly. "Shoot me. Make it look like another suicide. I'm sure the police will buy that. First Wendt kills himself, then me. That won't look too suspicious, will it? Only this time, Butch, they'll find your name and your beeper number among my personal effects."

"So what? That wouldn't mean anything."

"They'll also hear from the person who gave me that number."

"I'll take my chances," said Butch, deciding to call Michael's bluff.

"So will I," Michael replied without a trace of fear.

Neither man blinked for what seemed like an eternity. Frustrated, Butch finally lowered and uncocked his weapon. "Is this the thanks I get for avenging your wife's murder?" he demanded. "Hmm? You're screwing me out of $10,000. Is that my reward?"

"No one's screwing you out of anything. I gave you …"

"You were the judge and jury!" cried Butch. "I was just the executioner. You supplied the verdict and I carried out *your* sentence. You got what you wanted, goddamn it!" he insisted. "You got what you wanted."

"No," Michael denied. "No, I didn't. I came to my senses. I tried to prevent it."

"That doesn't make you any less guilty."

"Oh yes, it does," Michael firmly declared. "My conscience is clear. What you did ... you did of your own volition."

None of this sat well with Butch, but he realized that he didn't have any options. What was worse was that he knew that Michael knew it, too. He was unaccustomed to feeling helpless. It was humiliating and if there was one thing that Butch could not afford to tolerate, it was humiliation. "You have 24 hours to come up with the cash," he blurted with what little remaining bravado he could muster.

"Or what?" Michael countered. "You'll go to the police?"

Butch glared, but it was all he could do.

"Listen to me carefully," said Michael. "You have $10,000 of my money. That's more than you deserve. Consider yourself lucky."

Sure, thought Butch. *That's me — lucky. I hardly got to touch that cash before I had to turn it over, and I'm still up to my neck in debt. What does this Ivy League-educated prick know about luck?*

"Now get out of my home," Michael ordered. "And don't you ever, *ever* contact me again."

Butch smiled, tucked his gun in his belt and zipped up his leather jacket. "Okay, Mikey," he replied softly. "Have it your way."

Michael watched him walk out the door, then rushed to lock it. He took a deep breath and noticed that his hands were shaking. Nevertheless, he felt proud of myself and relieved. Finally, the nightmare was over. Now he was free to start fresh and put this all behind him. Everything was going to be fine, he assured himself. Just fine.

XVII

————————————————

Carlo Torello was not what one would call a patient man. He couldn't stand waiting for anything whether it was a movie ticket, a bank teller or a box of cannolis. He was just as restless when it came to interminable anecdotes and explanations that always seemed to end with "so, to make a long story short." But worst of all, Carlo hated waiting for money.

Of course, in his line of work, late payments were far and few between because they often resulted in hefty penalties – physically as well as financially. For example, there was the licensed electrician from Jersey City who ran up $45,000 in IOUs gambling on college basketball games, then conceded that he could only cover half of his losing bets. Two broken ribs, a ruptured spleen and multiple contusions later, he signed over his RV, sold 200 shares of Coca Cola and hocked all his gold jewelry – including his wedding ring – to appease Carlo and his humorless associates.

Thankfully, such extreme measures were usually unnecessary. At six foot, four inches tall, three hundred and fifty pounds, and with a face only a mother could love, Torello was an effectively intimidating figure. His connections were just as formidable, commanding the appropriate amount of fear and respect from his regular clientele. Only once in awhile did Carlo have to stoop to strong-arm tactics and make an example of some pathetic, down-on-his-luck deadbeat. But it never went *too* far. After all, you can't collect from a corpse. It was always more prudent and profitable to discourage tardiness with the threat of pain and suffering.

Not that Torello didn't cut some slack from time to time. Close friends – the precious few that he had – deserved at least a week or two to raise cash and make good on their markers. But then, any friend of Carlo's had the resources to win or lose big, and they knew that he had to answer to a higher authority. It was rare that he had to explain the time-honored principles of successful bookmaking to an errant debtor: You win, you collect. You lose, I collect. You lose and you can't pay me right away, you owe me interest. You owe me and you *still* don't pay me, then you'll wish that you had. But when it was incumbent of Carlo to press the matter, it was usually done at a cordial rendezvous in a public place – not unlike the friendly meeting he arranged with Butch at Angelo's restaurant.

Carlo and Butch went way back – at least 30 years. They were once affiliated with the same prominent Brooklyn family. That was until the Feds lowered the boom and upset the applecart. Their fathers belonged to the same crew and Butch and Carlo used to break bread at the same holiday and wedding tables. Once they even shared a box at Belmont racetrack for a couple of seasons, although they weren't exactly what you'd call *compadres*. Torello still belonged to the same social club in Sheepshead Bay, serving as a mid-level capo for a new generation, but now Butch was a freelancer working all sides of the street – as long as there were no serious conflicts of interest.

There were still strong ties between them, intangible debts and personal favors, as well as a history, that were important parts of the equation – factors that made their current state of affairs all the more delicate. Nevertheless, business was business and it didn't help matters that Butch was late for their appointment.

"Hey," he nodded, taking his seat at Carlo's table, neither offering his hand nor an apology or explanation for his tardiness.

"What's up?" asked Torello, dispensing with the usual pleasantries. "You got the rest of my money?"

"Soon," said Butch without blinking.

"Soon?" Torello grunted, determined not to lose his temper and send his blood pressure soaring. "How soon?"

"Real soon."

Torello rolled his tongue in his cheek and spoke with his hands. "Days, weeks, months ... what? Give me a fuckin' idea. Okay?"

Butch glanced over to the bar and recognized two of Carlo's men having a beer.

He wondered if Torello traveled with an entourage these days or if he had deliberately brought them along to deliver a less than subtle message. "I can't," he honestly replied. "Maybe tomorrow, maybe next week."

"*Maybe*?"

"What do you want me to say, Carlo? Huh? I'm not positive. I'm not going to yank your chain by making a promise I'm not sure I can keep."

"Gee, thanks. That's considerate of you," said Torello sarcastically.

"I'm waiting for a payment of my own," Butch elaborated. "As soon as I get my money, you'll get yours."

"Yeah, where have I heard that before ..."

"For Christ's sake, Carlo. It's not the first time I was late."

"Bingo. That's the fuckin' point."

"Gimme a break," Butch scoffed. "Whenever I owed you money, you always got paid."

"Yeah," Carlo conceded, "when you were good and ready."

"Big deal. So I stretched it out a little. You've got the best action this side of the Verranzano. It's not like you're hurtin' for cash."

"That's beside the point. It's a matter of *respect*. I extend you credit, I expect you to extend me a little fuckin' courtesy. I don't appreciate being played for a chump. Not by you, not by anybody."

"Aw, fuck this ..." Butch muttered, rising to his feet.

"Sit down," Torello ordered.

Butch smirked and turned to leave. But Carlo reached out and grabbed his arm tightly. The two enforcers at the bar lunged a few steps forward, but paused as Carlo held up his other hand. Butch glanced at the huge fist wrapped around his forearm. "Sit down," said Torello. Butch tugged, but Torello jerked him back. "Sit ... the fuck ... down," he quietly and sternly repeated.

The two men stared at each other while onlookers at nearby

tables watched curiously. Thinking better of an abrupt exit, Butch took his seat and Torello relinquished his grip.

"You know what your problem is?" asked Torello.

"No," Butch smugly replied, "but I got a feeling you're gonna' tell me."

"You've got expensive tastes. You like your high-priced toys with all the bells and whistles. You like your fine food and fancy wines ... your designer clothes and your Park Avenue whores. And God knows, you like the ponies."

"We all have our vices, Carlo." Butch dryly asserted.

"But we can't always afford them. The bitter truth is that you live way beyond your means, which is fine with me ... except when it affects my bottom line. Because that, my friend, is unacceptable."

"You know I'm good for the money," Butch insisted.

"If you were good for the money," Carlo retorted, "you would have paid me by now instead of putting us both in this embarrassing position."

Butch threw up his hands. "What am I supposed to do? Huh? Sell my fucking house?"

"That's not a bad idea. You live alone. You got no family left to support. What do you need with all that space, anyway? You could be living just as nicely but cheaper in one of those high-rise apartments on the river. At least scale down a little. Why don't you sell that Porsche of yours? Get something more affordable – like a goddamn Camry. I bet that would put a little green in your pocket."

"What are you," Butch laughed contemptuously, "my financial advisor?"

"This ain't funny, pal," said Torello, his face as hard as granite, his puffy eyes dark and piercing. "I've been more than patient with you, but my patience has reached its limit. This isn't the first or the second or even the third time that I've had to deal with your bullshit. But it *is* the last time," he warned ominously. "I don't care what you have to do, or who you have to do it to, but you'd better do it and do it fast." He held up his finger. "One more week. That's all I'm giving you."

"And then what?" Butch wondered aloud, pressing his luck. Carlo shrugged. "Then I stop asking."

Without further adieu, Torello lifted his portly frame from his seat and shuffled off. His two apes finished their drinks at the bar and followed him, leaving Butch to weigh his options. There weren't many to consider – just one, in fact. Some unfinished business that needed to be resolved.

XVIII

Since his divorce, Alan Davis would often spend his Friday or Saturday nights at Paladin, a ritzy restaurant with an adjacent cocktail lounge located in the quaint, upscale town of Ridgewood, New Jersey. There, bellying up to the bar on the fringe of a parquet dance floor, he could anesthetize the pain of a failed marriage with a potent prescription of vodka martinis and whiskey sours while flirting the night away with a bevy of lovelorn divorcees and confirmed career bachelorettes.

At approximately 10 p.m., he would drive up to the curb in his powder blue BMW, hand his car keys to the valet and eagerly retreat to a world of bluesy ballads, meaningful gazes and raging pheromones. Bypassing the dining area and the maitre d's station, Alan would proceed directly to the barroom where mostly professional men and women in their thirties, forties and fifties would congregate for the suburban mating ritual. Dressed to the nines, oozing with charm and virtually reeking of Drakkar, Alan would unashamedly flaunt his success, whatever would entice a lonely female to his side, to the dance floor or, occasionally, to his bed.

With his male pattern baldness and less than charismatic looks, he knew he was no prize, no matinee idol. But then most of the eligible females who frequented Paladin weren't looking for perfection, nor even superficial attractiveness. It was his mere availability, combined with his intellectual cache, his perceived savoir-faire, and, certainly, his lucrative occupation that would suffice – if only for one night.

"Me? I'm a financial advisor for a Wall Street brokerage firm," he would casually reveal at the circular bar, noting the keen interest such a disclosure would elicit in a potential conquest's eyes. "My clients include various recording artists on the Columbia, Arista and Atlantic labels, some professional athletes, and quite a few Fortune 500 corporate executives," he would nonchalantly add to impress. If Alan had learned anything as a single man, it was that money and prestige were greater aphrodisiacs than good looks and a full head of hair.

It also helped if one were a competent dancer. The dance floor at Paladin was relatively small and always crowded, but Alan used it to his best advantage. Adventurous ladies rarely declined an invitation, and if they did there was always more where they came from. Even under these awkward circumstances, pressing flesh with a virtual stranger was a relatively harmless, romantic escape, a welcome departure from the harsh reality of their stressful, loveless lives. Accustomed to the house band's playlist, Alan's modus operandi was to lure an unwitting acquaintance to the floor with a harmless, touchless rocker that was immediately followed by an embraceable slow dance. With no excuse to sit out a quiet number, the unsuspecting partner would submissively follow Alan's lead, surrendering to the comfort of his enfolding arms, incrementally seduced by his subtly sinful, groin grinding moves.

It often amazed and delighted Alan that there were so many fine, available women in the world who craved affection. And yet, there was something inescapably bittersweet, sometimes sad, about the whole dating scene. In his more wistful, self-pitying moments, he felt like one of the lonely people inhabiting *Eleanor Rigby*, doomed to spend eternity haunting places like this, chatting up perennial bridesmaids, scoring with but never connecting with anyone he could honestly call his soul mate. Well, he thought philosophically, it could be worse. At least he wasn't a widower like Michael. Now *that* had to be unbearable. Although, who was to say which was worse – losing a loved one or losing a loved one's love?

Regardless of his dance partner, Alan's thoughts would invariably wander into memories of his ex-wife Heather. He would recall all the occasions when they had danced together – all the wedding receptions and bar mitzvahs they had attended as man and wife – how happy they had looked in all the photographs that were now stored away in boxes in a utility closet. The goofy, big-toothed grins. The cheek-to-cheek embraces as if nothing could ever separate them. Ha! All it took was a few years of Alan's insatiable workaholism and Heather's extravagance to drive a stake through the heart of that relationship. Heather's affair with one of Alan's former business associates didn't help, either. Such were the shallow depths of their commitment and tolerance. Fortunately, there had been no children – just property that could be claimed and divided with a modicum of civility. Still ... Alan knew that if he hadn't been so proud and Heather had been just a little more flexible, it might have worked out. Sometimes, even as he was embellishing his personal and professional resume for some wide-eyed, would-be lover, he wished that it had.

But this Saturday night was less than promising. Hardly any of the unescorted women at Paladin were Alan's type, just an odd assortment of middle-aged, born-again swingers and all-too-familiar, burnt-out regulars. Or was it he who was burnt-out, played out, and in need of a change of venue? After a few drinks and a few provocative glances, he realized the futility of his weekend exercise. Conceding boredom, he left a $10 tip for his favorite barmaid and headed for the door.

Alan was legally intoxicated, but had no apprehension about getting behind the wheel of his vehicle. The ride home to Upper Saddle River would be a short one and he knew enough to take it nice and easy to avoid being pulled over by Bergen County's finest. Keeping his steering wheel steady and watching his speed, he took Paramus Road north and then veered west, climbing the winding, rustic foothills that led to his two-story, red brick house.

Along the way, he cracked a window and let the chilly evening breeze invigorate his senses. He restlessly surfed the radio scanner for a song that didn't depress, annoy or insult his intelligence, but came up empty. Naturally, he had recently tidied up the interior of his vehicle and neglected to restock it with his favorite CDs. It didn't really matter. Nothing could have drowned out his thoughts, anyway. He was contemplating the next 40 or 50 years of his life, years that either would be spent utterly alone or making the same mistakes over and over again. Given the improbability of living happily ever after, Alan didn't see the point in investing time in a meaningful relationship. The first several months would be magically blissful, the next few years challenging, and the rest a lingering, litigious nightmare. No more Heathers for him. But then ... what? A lifetime of managing other people's money? A long series of inevitable disappointments. And then ...

Lighten up for Christ's sake, Alan chided himself as he pulled into his driveway, turned off his headlights, and silenced the engine. *So you didn't get laid tonight. At least you made it home safe and sound.* He would have parked the car in his garage, but it was filled with boxes, furniture and appliances – Heather's crap, things she didn't have room for in her apartment and he had graciously agreed to store, as well as things she simply didn't want anymore but he couldn't bear to part with – the stuff that poignant memories are made of. Banishing the thought from his weary mind, he stepped out of his car, slammed the door and locked it with his remote. Then he trudged up the walkway and turned the corner toward the front door.

It happened very quickly – the snap of a twig, a fleeting shadow, Alan reflexively turning on his heels, receiving the stunning blow of a blunt instrument as unexpected and devastating as a bolt of lightning. The force of impact was so powerful that it lifted Alan off his feet and sent him sprawling onto his back several feet away. There he laid on the wet carpet of his lawn, the front of his skull fractured to such a degree that it triggered an instantly fatal cerebral hemorrhage. As it is often said of such unforeseen circumstances, he never knew what hit him.

"Wow," Butch remarked, marveling at his own strength. "Now that's what I call gettin' whacked."

The Louisville slugger bat in his gloved hands was cracked, but intact and stainless. No blood had been splattered. Another plus: The full-acre property was set back from the main road, the nearest neighbor at least five hundred feet away. No likely witnesses. So far, so good. Still, Butch wasted no time retrieving Alan's key chain, unlocking the BMW and dragging the body to the passenger side. With a swift heave-ho he propped Alan in the front seat, got in on the driver's side, rested the bat against his leg and turned on the ignition.

As he drove along the dark, twisting backroads, Butch sardonically addressed his lifeless victim. "So," he said, glancing to his right. "How's the technology sector these days? I'm thinking of investing in a mutual fund. Got any recommendations for me?"

He paused, as if waiting for a response. "Hm?" Butch asked, his playful eyes shifting from the road to Alan to the road again. "What's the matter? Cat got your tongue?"

Alan's battered head bobbed like a rag doll's as the wheels bounced with the occasional pothole. "From what I heard, you were very good at foreseeing sudden shifts in the market," said Butch. "Too bad you didn't foresee this, huh? But that's what you get for becoming involved in somebody else's vendetta. I just want you to know that this isn't personal. I guess you could say that I've got a low risk tolerance and I'm just looking out for my investments. You know what I mean?"

A few minutes later, Butch parked the car on the shoulder of a nearby thoroughfare closed for construction and left the engine running. He got out, bat in hand, and hurled the murder weapon over a steep ravine and into the thicket of a wooded area below. He then moved aside one of the construction barriers that blocked the road and returned to the vehicle. He hastily transferred Alan to the driver's seat, carefully remembering to buckle his seat belt. Leaning through the open window, he shifted the car into drive and turned the steering wheel slightly to the left. Running alongside the vehicle for about a hundred feet, Butch made sure it veered onto the pavement, building speed as it coasted downhill. Eventually he leaped clear of the car and watched as it hurtled toward a sharp curve in the road. By the time it crossed the yellow line, the vehicle had accelerated to forty miles per hour. Seconds later, it smashed through a cable guardrail and careened through bushes and trees down a 75-foot embankment. Judging by the resonating sound of the crash, the car was totally demolished. Fortunately, there was no ensuing explosion or fire. It all but guaranteed that the wreck would not be discovered for quite a few hours.

Not one to stick around and admire his work, Butch inconspicuously headed back toward Alan's house on foot, concealing himself on the side of the road only once from the glaring headlights of a passing SUV. It took him twenty minutes to get back to the original scene of the crime, but when he got there he found his Porsche where he had left it across the road, parked behind a cluster of evergreen trees.

As he drove south and east, Butch listened to the sweet, quiet purr of his engine and savored the moment. With one bold stroke, he had eliminated the only link between himself and Michael Gray. He had also taken a decisive step toward obtaining what was rightfully his. He was, after all, a man of action. Nobody could screw him and get away with it, certainly no candy-ass, yuppie book editor.

For the rest of the night, Butch wore the smile of a man who had it all figured out. Alan Davis's death would be ruled an accident. Toxicology tests would reveal that he was legally intoxicated at the time of death. Apparently, he had taken a wrong turn, lost control of his vehicle and was killed by a massive blow to the forehead sustained in the ensuing crash. As they used to say in his old neighborhood, end of story.

Of course, Butch still had some unfinished business – but not for long.

XIX

Of all the mourners at Alan's funeral, Michael seemed to be taking it the hardest. After what he had been through over the past two years, there were no tears left in him. But while others were merely stunned by Alan's sudden and inexplicable demise, Michael's grief was palpable, threatening to plunge him back into the melancholic depths he had only recently crawled out of. First he lost Karen, now his best friend, both dying violently and long before their time. This wasn't the way it was supposed to be. They were all going to live happily and successfully ever after – he and Karen, Alan and Heather. Wasn't it enough that Michael had endured one devastating loss? Apparently, not. Just when he thought his life was turning around for the better, Michael was beset with another senseless, inconceivable tragedy. Was this God's way of punishing him for his involvement in Leon Wendt's murder?

Listen to yourself, thought Michael, watching Heather, garbed in black, as she stood stoically but teary-eyed over Alan's flower-draped casket. *How do you think she feels – regardless of the divorce*? Or Alan's parents, sisters and brother for that matter?

No one, especially not Alan, had expected it to end this way or this soon. Sure, he had been a little reckless at times, a little too self-indulgent for his own good. But he wasn't stupid enough to drive drunk down an abandoned roadway and off a cliff. If Alan, like Karen, could die so easily, so senselessly, so young, what hope was there for anyone else?

As the Davis family's rabbi read aloud a kaddish from his prayer book, Michael scanned the reverent faces of those gathered around the gravesite. He recognized more than half of them as relatives and friends of the deceased. The rest were probably co-workers at Alan's brokerage firm or long-standing clients, such as the tall, brawny African-American man Michael recognized as a linebacker for the New York Giants. Or was it the Jets? He looked so solemn and sensitive with his head bowed and his hands folded in front of him. But then he shifted his weight from one leg to the other and Michael thought he caught a glimpse of someone else over his shoulder in the distance – a familiar, gray-haired man in a black leather jacket.

Michael audibly gasped, drawing the attention of those immediately around him. Embarrassed, he sheepishly avoided their curious stares and looked down at his shoes. But it was hard to conceal his shock and sudden anxiety. He respectfully waited until the prayer ended, then murmured, "Excuse me," abruptly extricating himself from the crowd.

It was a clear, sunny, windswept day. Yet, as he surveyed the sprawling landscape of the cemetery, Michael felt a deep, numbing chill. He tucked his hands into his overcoat pockets and began to walk. Rambling from plot to plot through the morbid maze of monuments and crypts, Michael searched in vain for the elusive man in the black leather jacket. He would catch a fleeting glimpse of something in the corner of his eye, only to turn and see nothing but row upon row of headstones. Then the breeze, like a taunting whisper, would tap him on the shoulder and he would reel around, simply to realize that he was alone, that he had strayed too far from his party, that he was surely lost. Had his eyes deceived him? Or was he merely haunted by his guilt? Would Butch have the audacity to appear at Alan's funeral? And why would he do such a thing? Unless ...

Michael paused in his tracks and glanced down at a marble plaque at his feet. Judging by the names, it was dedicated to the memories of a relatively young woman and her two adolescent children. Oddly, the exact date of their deaths was the same. What was *their* story? Did they perish together in a fire? Did they drown in icy waters? What unforeseen circumstances had claimed their lives?

Then Michael looked up at the sky above the stark, looming trees and a realization came to him like a bolt of lightning. *Oh, God, no*, he shuddered.

****

The plan had been to take the rest of the day off to sit *shivah* with Alan's family in their Brooklyn Heights duplex. But instead, Michael took a cab into Manhattan and rushed to his office. He tried to as inconspicuous as possible and not look frantic, slowing his pace as he exited the elevator and strode through the corridors of the editorial division.

"Michael ..."Angela declared as she turned a corner, surprised to see him.

"What are you doing here today?"

"I just ... have a few things to take care of," he claimed, sidestepping his assistant. "I'm not staying."

"Anything I can help you with?" Angela offered as Michael kept moving.

"No, thanks," he replied over his shoulder.

Once inside his office, Michael threw off his overcoat and immediately began rifling through the drawers of his desk searching for a certain piece of paper. As soon as he found it, he reached for the phone. But before he could press any of the numbers scribbled on the slip, he glanced up and was startled to see Cynthia standing in the doorway. "Oh ... hi," said Michael, replacing the telephone receiver on its cradle.

"May I speak with you?" asked Cynthia, looking rather pensive.

Michael balked but resisted the urge to ask her if it could wait. "Sure," he replied less than enthusiastically.

Cynthia closed the door behind her, which warned Michael that he was in for an earful. Bracing himself, he stashed the paper in his pocket, rose and walked around to the front of the desk to confront her.

"I think ... we made a mistake," said Cynthia. "I mean ... *I* made a mistake by sleeping with you."

Michael stared at her, bewildered. "Why do you think that?"

Cynthia sighed and glanced at the ceiling. "Michael, it's been more than a week since we went out. You haven't asked me out again. You haven't called me. You've barely spoken to me since we ..."

Not now, *not now*, thought Michael. "I'm sorry," he apologized. "I really am. It's just that ..."

"I know, I know," Cynthia interrupted. "You're not ready for a relationship. I understand. We were too impulsive ..."

"No, no. It's not that," Michael insisted with a dismissive gesture. "Really. I had a ... a personal problem I had to deal with and then ..."he added, realizing that a vague explanation would not suffice. "Well ... my best friend was killed in a car accident. I just came from the funeral."

"Oh, dear," Cynthia shuddered sympathetically. "I'm so sorry. I had no idea ... Are you alright?"

"Yes, of course," Michael lied. "I'm fine. It's just ... it's been a crazy week. I'm sorry if I've been missing in action. But I wasn't avoiding you, if that's what you think." To reassure her, Michael took Cynthia in his arms and gave her a hug. "I'm sorry," he said softly in her ear.

"Are you sure it's just that?" asked Cynthia. "I mean … if things got too intense between us too soon, we could always …"

"Everything is fine between us," Michael insisted.

Still doubtful, Cynthia nevertheless clung to him. "Am I going to see you again?" she asked. "Away from the office, that is."

"Of course," Michael promised, gently pulling away and placing his hand affectionately against her cheek. "Of course we'll see each other," he laughed. "What sort of guy do you think I am?"

"Oh, Michael ..."Cynthia moaned, her imploring eyes begging for sincerity.

"We'll do something next weekend. I promise. Just give me a few days to sort things out."

"I'll give you all the time you need," said Cynthia. "Just be honest with me. Okay?"

Michael forced a smile and nodded. "Okay."

"You must be going through hell. Is there anything I can do for you?"

"No."

"Are you *sure*?"

Michael bit his lip, trying not to betray his impatience. "Yes, I'm sure. If I need anything ..." Rather than finishing his sentence, Michael impulsively leaned forward and kissed Cynthia on the lips, taking her by surprise. He knew that's what she wanted, that it would please and reassure her. He may have been out of practice, but there were certain things about appeasing women he hadn't forgotten. "Now, if don't mind ..." he said delicately, trying not to sound as if he were abruptly dismissing her. "I need to make an important phone call."

Cynthia caught her breath and backed away slowly. "Well," she smiled, opening the door. "You know where to find me."

As soon as Cynthia left, Michael returned to his desk and reached for the phone. Disoriented, he forgot where he had put the number, stressfully combing his desktop and drawers without success. Finally, he remembered and retrieved the piece of paper fromhis pocket. Nervously, he pounded Butch's beeper number and held his breath waiting for it to ring. Instead, he got a recording: "We're sorry, but the number you have called is no longer in service." He tried it again, but with the same result.

Michael put down the phone and slumped into his chair. He wanted to believe that Butch had nothing to do with Alan's death, that he wasn't at the funeral and that he was out of his life forever. But what Michael wanted to believe and what he feared were two different things. Lately, everything he feared sooner or later became reality. And with no way to contact Butch, all Michael could do was wait for Butch to contact him. Wait and wonder where and when ... and how.

XX

Cynthia worked overtime that evening, determined to meet a self-imposed deadline on the latest Bruce Chafey manuscript. The great thing about editing Chafey books was that they were always real page-turners. Even in first draft they provided a brisk tailwind that helped move the project smoothly and swiftly to publication. They were also effectively terrifying with their assortment of fiendish characters, grisly murders, eerie settings and suspenseful plot twists – the stuff of which the seeds of nightmares were easily sown in the impressionable subconscious of a single woman living alone in the big city.

Cynthia had become so absorbed in her reading that she was truly surprised when she glanced at her wristwatch and discovered it was nearly 9:30 p.m. Everyone else in Editorial had long since gone home; even the maintenance workers had completed their rounds of vacuuming carpets and emptying wastebaskets. So Cynthia reluctantly filed away the manuscript, gathered her belongings and called it a day, switching off lights along the way to the exit.

At the elevator bank, she pressed the down button and waited patiently, thinking about all the chores that awaited her when she got home. If she were lucky, she would get to sleep by one a.m., only to wake up in six hours and repeat the whole daily grind. One would think that, at this hour, the elevator would arrive immediately. Naturally, that was not the case. Perhaps, thought Cynthia, there was only one of three elevators in service after hours. Impatient, she pressed the down button again. "Come on," she muttered restlessly, tapping her toe against the closed elevator doors. Then she sighed and slowly turned around, flinching at the sight of another person who had been standing behind her.

He was a moderately tall man in his forties, brawny from the waist up and slender from the waist down. He had thick gray hair, piercing blue eyes and a frighteningly conspicuous scar on the left side of his neck. He was wearing a black leather jacket, blue jeans and imported black boots – obviously not an employee of Paragon Books. Startled and self-conscious, Cynthia acknowledged him with a false, fleeting smile, then turned her back without saying a word.

Perhaps it was the result of reading too much Bruce Chafey, combined with her New Yorker paranoia, but Cynthia was anything but comfortable with this situation. Who was this guy, she wondered, and what was he doing here after nine o'clock at night?

The important question, of course, was what to do next. There seemed to be three options: act fearlessly and get on the elevator with him, feign impatience and head for the nearest staircase, or pretend to have forgotten something in her office and catch the next elevator. As far as Cynthia could tell, there was no one left on the floor who could come to her aid if this guy turned out to be trouble. So she immediately ruled out returning to the office. It would certainly be foolish to risk being followed into a stairwell. At least the elevator had a video surveillance camera and an emergency button. She had also taken a few classes in self-defense. Of course, that was a couple of years ago and she scarcely remembered a thing she had learned.

Cynthia flinched again as the elevator tone abruptly chimed and the doors slid open. She hesitated for a moment, staring into the empty car, then reluctantly stepped aboard, followed by the stranger. Cynthia positioned herself next to the console, while the stranger leaned against the opposite wall. The elevator doors remained open until she impulsively jabbed the close button. Finally, the doors closed slowly, confining them in their metal box.

There was an uneasy moment of silence during which Cynthia detected the enticing scent of men's cologne – Channel's Allure Homme, if she wasn't mistaken – mingled with a subtle stench of nicotine. The tension was so thick that it took her several seconds to realize that the elevator wasn't moving. Suddenly, Cynthia caught movement in the corner of her eye. *The stranger was lunging toward her.* She gasped and turned to confront him, but watched as he merely reached over to press the lobby button, which she had neglected to press herself. As the elevator started its descent, the stone-faced stranger returned to his spot and folded arms across his chest. Embarrassed, Cynthia faced forward again, looked down at her shoes and bit her lip. *He must think I'm a real nutcase*, she chided herself.

But when Cynthia's eyes drifted up, she noticed something unsettling in the convex mirror in the corner of the ceiling – the stranger was staring at her. She looked straight ahead at the emergency button and counted the floors as the elevator descended at what seemed like a snail's pace. Still, she could feel his white hot gaze, scrutinizing her from head to toe, leeringly lingering below her waist, detailing the supple curves of her hips, derriere and shapely calves. Cynthia's palms began to sweat, her heart palpitating. Why was this nonstop elevator ride taking so damn long? And why wasn't she carrying a can of pepper spray in her handbag like she used to when she had been a co-ed at Sarah Lawrence. *Hold on*, she told herself. *Don't panic. You'll be out of here in a moment. Focus on the emergency button.*

Finally, the elevator arrived at the main floor. As soon as the doors opened, Cynthia sprang like a racehorse breaking from the starting gate. She headed straight for the lobby's security desk, but when she turned the corner she found no one there. A nearby newstand was closed, as well. She looked around, searching in vain for anyone who might be loitering in the lobby. Then she glanced over her shoulder and saw the stranger sauntering toward her slowly. He was still staring at her with the slightest trace of a smile on his lips, sending a chill down Cynthia's spine.

She kept moving, her heels clicking briskly as she quickly crossed the lobby, whirled through a set of revolving doors, and escaped onto Madison Avenue. At the curb, she tried hailing a cab, but to no avail. She looked back and there was the stranger, lingering at the building entrance and watching her as he casually lit a cigarette.

Knowing she was relatively safe on the well-lit and bustling city streets, Cynthia started walking. If he continued to follow her, she could always flag down a police car or duck into a coffee shop and call for help. That would put an abrupt end to this silly little cat-and-mouse game.

Sure enough, after she had walked a few blocks, Cynthia's fears were allayed. She paused in front of a fashion boutique and pretended to be window-shopping. Glancing in the direction from which she had come, she confirmed the disappearance of her mysterious stalker. Relieved, she briskly proceeded east to the nearest Lexington Avenue subway station.

Ordinarily, Cynthia would stand in the middle of the platform while waiting for the uptown train. That was where most of the passengers usually congregated. At this hour of the evening, however, the station was virtually deserted. So Cynthia wandered further down the platform and took a seat on a bench to rest her feet. Leaning her head back, she closed her weary eyes for a moment. She listened to the haunting howl of the wind as it rushed through the subway tunnels, the distant thunder of trains rumbling through intersecting routes, the thumping bass of a fleeting hip-hop song and the faint but steady hum of city traffic through the sidewalk grating above. She also heard the distinct sounds of a rotating turnstile and a pair of boots heels clacking on concrete. It compelled her to open her eyes and peer down the platform, where she catch a chilling glimpse of the gray-haired stranger's profile.

Quietly but promptly, Cynthia rose from her seat and sought concealment behind a pillar near the edge of the platform. Surely this was not a coincidence. He must have followed her to the station unnoticed. Now what was she supposed to do? She was too far down the platform to elude him. She couldn't exit the station without crossing his path. And if she boarded the next train, she might end up alone with him in the car. Or he could follow her home, find out where she lived and God knows what else. *Why was this happening?* Cynthia fretted. What did he want? And where the hell was a transit cop when you needed one?

Cynthia simply decided to stay put and out of sight. Hidden from view, she would wait to see if he got on the next train. If he did, she would wait for another or walk all the way home if she still couldn't find a cab. *Just keep calm, be quiet, and don't panic,* she told herself.

But then Cynthia heard the stranger's telltale footsteps on the move again. They sounded as if they were getting louder, closer. He was slowly heading in her direction. With her back against the narrow pillar, she tried desperately not to be seen, clutching her handbag to her chest, fearfully conscious of her heavy breathing. Judging by the sound of his wandering boot heels, he was about twenty-five to thirty feet away and still approaching. Each step grew louder and louder – twenty feet away, fifteen. *Goddamn it, where was the train?*

Then the footsteps ceased. Everything was unnervingly still. Cynthia held her breath for what seemed like an eternity, not knowing what to expect. Frozen to the spot, she could *hear* her own rapid heartbeat and felt as if her lungs would burst. Then she heard the footsteps again, only now they were slowly retreating, gradually drowned out by the rising reverberation of an approaching train. When the noise reached its crescendo, Cynthia finally exhaled and took another deep breath. The train screeched to a halt and its doors slid open. Taking a chance, Cynthia peered from the edge of the pillar to see the gray-haired stranger board one of the cars and flop into a seat. While she watched, the doors closed and the train, carrying her suspected stalker, left the station without her.

Too stressed to linger, Cynthia headed for the nearest exit. Back on Lexington Avenue, she stood on a corner for ten minutes until she was finally able to stop a cab. "85th between Second and Third," she told the taxi driver, then settled back in her seat for a gloriously bumpy and breakneck ride uptown.

As they approached their destination, Cynthia leaned forward to provide the driver with the exact location of her apartment building. When he slowed his vehicle, however, she spotted someone standing directly across the street from the brownstone.

"Don't stop," she abruptly instructed.

"Huh?" the cabbie replied.

"Don't stop! Keep driving!" Cynthia snapped, slouching down

to avoid being seen by the gray-haired stranger waiting for her to arrive home.

"Lady ..." said the driver. "What the ..."

"I changed my mind," said Cynthia. "I have another address I want you to take me to."

****

Michael was more than surprised to see Cynthia at his door. One look at her face and he knew something was terribly wrong.

"Hi," she said. "I'm sorry to disturb you at this hour."

"That's all right," he replied. "Are you okay? Is anything wrong?"

"Can I come in?"

"Of course," said Michael, opening the door wider and standing aside.

Cynthia entered the alcove and apologized again. "Forgive me. I didn't know where else to go."

Michael locked the door behind her, took Cynthia by the arm and led her into the living room. "Here ... give me your coat. Would you like something to drink? You look like you could use it."

"No, thanks," said Cynthia, sitting down on the sofa. "I just need to collect myself. I'm a little shaken."

"What happened?"

Cynthia hesitated, fighting back tears. "Someone followed me home from work tonight," said Cynthia.

Michael gaped at her. "What do you mean ... followed you?"

"A man ..."she said in a quivering voice. "He got on the elevator with me. He was staring at me. Then ... then he followed me to the subway ..." Cynthia paused to dab her eyes with a Kleenex. "I managed to lose him," she continued, controlling her emotions, "and took a cab to my place, but he was waiting for me there. He was across the street, waiting for me to come home."

"Did he do anything?" asked Michael. "Did he say anything to you?"

"No. And I didn't say anything to him. I was too afraid to confront him. But I know he was following me."

"What did he look like?"

Cynthia sighed. "He was about your height. Not old, but he had gray hair. He had blue eyes. And ... and he had a big scar on his neck," she added, drawing a diagonal line with her finger along the left side of her throat. "What is it, Michael? You look pale."

"No, I ... I'm just concerned ... for you," he stammered, sitting down beside Cynthia and taking her hand.

"I'm okay," she insisted. "Really. I was just frightened. Wherever I went, he went. Then, when I saw him across the street from my building, I didn't want to get out of the cab and be alone in my apartment. That's why I came here."

"I don't blame you."

"Should I have called the police?" asked Cynthia.

"No!" Michael said too abruptly. "I mean ... what good would that have done?"

"They could have held him for questioning."

"Nah. He'd have fled at the first sight of a cop," Michael scoffed. "He was probably just some creep who was attracted to you or something. I doubt you'll ever see him again."

"But he knew where I lived," Cynthia observed. "But then, if he knew where I lived, why was he following me from work?" she wondered.

"Are you sure you saw him outside your apartment?"

"I thought I did."

"Maybe you were just so upset that you imagined it was him," Michael rationalized.

Cynthia ran her fingers through her hair in frustration. "Oh, I don't know. I was just so scared."

"It's okay now," Michael said reassuringly, taking Cynthia into his arms.

"Everything's going to be all right. You did the right thing by coming here."

"Did I? I won't stay long," she promised.

"Nonsense," said Michael. "Spend the night. You can have my bed."

"With or without you in it?" Cynthia murmured in his ear.

"That's entirely up to you," Michael replied, tenderly pressing his lips to her forehead and stroking her hair.

Looking over his shoulder, Cynthia noticed several framed photographs of Karen displayed throughout the room. "She was beautiful," she said.

"Who?" asked Michael.

"Your wife," Cynthia replied, motioning toward the photographs.

Michael slowly stood up, walked over to the bookcase and reached for his favorite portrait of Karen. "Yes, she was," he agreed.

"You must miss her very much," said Cynthia, trying to sound sympathetic rather than a tad jealous.

"I do," he conceded, studying the photo. "But then ..." He paused and returned the picture frame to its place. "... who wouldn't? She was very special. Smart as a whip. Funny. Kind. Compassionate. And very, very perceptive. Boy," he said, shaking his head, "she had me all figured out. I was your typical, callow, shallow boy when we met. But she turned me around," he smiled wistfully. After a long silence, Michael turned to Cynthia. "What else do you want to know?" he asked.

"Do you really believe that 'time heals all wounds?'" she adroitly inquired.

Michael took a moment to consider the question. "I don't know," he answered, staring bravely into Cynthia's eyes. "But I hope so."

Suddenly the phone rang, breaking the spell. "Excuse me," said Michael, taking the call in the bedroom.

"Hello?"

"How is she?" asked Butch, his deep, heartless voice making the hair on the back of Michael's neck stand on end. "Safe and sound?"

Michael was too startled to speak.

"What's the matter?" Butch goaded. "Got nothing to say to your old friend?"

"It was you, wasn't it?" Michael accused, keeping his voice as low as possible. "You were at the funeral today."

"Was I?"

"You were responsible for Alan's death, weren't you?"

"Not according to the coroner," Butch quipped.

"You son of a bitch ..."

"That's a lovely lady you've got there," declared Butch. "Pretty as a peach. We had an interesting evening together ..."

"What do you want?" Michael demanded.

"Oh, Mikey ... You know what I want. But just to make it abundantly clear, let's get together tomorrow. Shall we? We have a few things to discuss. 12:30. Pier 17 on 12th Avenue. Don't be late."

"Listen, you ..." But before Michael could continue, Butch hung up. Michael held the receiver to his ear until he heard a dial tone, then solemnly returned it to its cradle.

"Everything all right?" asked Cynthia when Michael returned to the living room.

"Yes. Fine," he lied, ignoring the doubtful suspicion in her eyes. "Wrong number," he claimed.

"At this hour?"

"How about that drink?" Michael suggested, changing the subject. "It'll calm your nerves."

"Okay," she relented, removing her coat. "But just one. I prefer to be sober when we make love."

Michael offered a smile that Cynthia interpreted as soulful. But inside, he burned with fear. Michael had had his share of dark moments in his life. But this one was the darkest of all.

XXI

"Are you sure this is it?" Michael asked doubtfully.

"Pier 17," the cab driver confirmed, switching off his meter.

Michael handed him a twenty-dollar bill. "Keep the change," he said and climbed out of the taxi.

It was a dreary, chilly day made gloomier by an on-again, off-again drizzle. It was even colder by the dilapidated docks along the Hudson River where a northwesterly wind gusted, forcing Michael to turn up his coat collar as he warily approached the abandoned loading facility. This was more clandestine than he had hoped, dangerously so. If he went inside, who could say for sure he would ever walk out? Yet what choice did he have?

The building's huge main entrance was sealed and barricaded, but there was a metal sidedoor that Michael found unlocked. Gingerly, he opened it and stepped inside.

It was some sort of empty warehouse that resembled an aircraft hangar with its long square footage, towering ceiling and lofty rafters. In this hollow musty shell his footsteps echoed as he drifted across the cement floor toward an area in the center of the interior illuminated by the daylight that poured through the broken pane of a skylight. There he paused and waited, sensing he was not alone.

"Well, well, well ..." came the voice Michael was expecting to hear. "If it isn't my old partner in crime."

Michael turned to his left. Butch emerged from the shadows

with his hands in his jacket pockets and a smug smirk on his face. "Didn't think you'd be seeing me again, did you?" he remarked.

"No," Michael admitted. "I was hoping ..."

"That I'd just go away," Butch interjected. "Disappear. Like waking up from a bad dream."

"Something like that."

"No such luck, smiley. Dream on ..."

"Why did you have to kill Alan?"

"I didn't," said Butch, pacing slowly, deliberately in a wide circle. "That was all *your* fault, Mikey. If you hadn't been so abrupt with me, so ... disrespectful, Alan would be alive today."

"Was that your motive?" asked Michael.

"That was part of it," Butch replied. "You threatened me, remember? You warned me that someone had brought us together. Once I found out who the middle man was, I had no choice but to eliminate him. I also wanted to get your attention ... if you catch my drift. Now that I have it, let me get to the point." He stopped pacing and looked directly at Michael. "I believe you owe me something."

Michael swallowed hard, summoning what was left of his courage. "I thought we had already resolved that."

"Well," sighed Butch. "You thought wrong. The last time we spoke, you acted as if you had the upper hand. But the fact of the matter, Mikey, is that you don't. At least not anymore. The game, my friend, is over."

Butch paused to light a cigarette. In the meantime, Michael said nothing, waiting for the rest of the pitch and the inevitable ultimatum.

"Here's the bottom line," Butch finally declared, exhaling billows of smoke and filling the air with its pungent aroma. "Neither one of us can go to the police, so there's no use playing that card. But, for argument's sake, let's say you were foolish enough to do so. I would take you down with me. And not only for Wendt. I'd tell them that you put me up to killing your friend Alan, too, to cover your tracks. It would be awfully hard to prove otherwise to a jury. You would do time. And a handsome, mild-mannered fellow like you would spend most of it on his knees or bent over a prison cot. So coming clean and throwing yourself on the mercy of the court is not an option." Butch took another drag. "Neither is negotiating a settlement."

"And why is that?" Michael wondered, regarding him askew.

"Because what happened to Alan could happen again."

"Are you threatening me?"

"Hell, no," Butch scoffed. "It's like you said, kill you and I won't collect a cent. No, Mikey. I wouldn't hurt you. But that pretty girlfriend of yours ..."

Michael's face turned ashen.

"Imagine that," said Butch with a delight he could hardly contain. "Losing *two* women in your life."

"You're insane ..."

"Then there's your dear mother up in Connecticut, your cousins in Tarrytown, your Aunt Mary in Great Neck ..."

"I'll give you the money," Michael conceded.

"What was that?" Butch taunted, putting a hand to his ear.

"I said, I'll give you the $10,000."

"Oh, that's another thing," said Butch, tapping his lips with his forefinger.

"I'm afraid there'll be a late payment charge."

"What?"

"You now owe me $20,000."

"I don't have that kind of money," said Michael.

"Oh, but I know you do," Butch replied, flicking ashes and moving closer. "You've got a good-paying job. You live in a nice apartment in the heart of Manhattan. I'll bet you even collected some insurance when your wife died. Come on, Mikey. Don't insult my intelligence."

"I'm telling you, I don't have $20,000 to give you," Michael insisted.

"Well, then, you'd better find a way to come up with it," warned Butch, jabbing Michael in the chest with his finger. "And you'd better come up with it fast. Because if you don't, you're going to be attending one funeral after another. Do you understand?"

Butch waited for an answer. When Michael failed to respond,

Butch tossed his cigarette aside, grabbed him by the lapels of his coat, and shoved him violently against a pillar. "Do you fucking understand me!" Butch roared in Michael face, his voice reverberating in their hollow sanctum.

Michael simply stared at him, unable to comprehend the depths of Butch's malevolence. "You're *mine*," he was gleefully informed. "Get used to it."

As the two men stared far into each other's eyes, however, Michael had a moment of clarity. Indeed, he understood. Perhaps too well. He saw beyond the payoff, beyond the feeble hope that an exchange of cash could possibly end this nightmare. He finally realized who and what he was dealing with. Like Leon Wendt, Butch was a cold, heartless killer, greedy and vindictive to the core. He would never be satisfied with another $20,000. As long as he had Michael where he wanted him, he would demand more. And more. And when the money ran out, there would be nothing to protect Michael from becoming the victim of an unfortunate accident of his own. There was only one other option.

"I'll call you within the next few days," said Butch. "When I do, be ready with the money." He let loose of Michael's threads and slowly backed away, returning to the shadows.

As soon as he heard the sidedoor slam shut, Michael rushed to the exit. Discreetly, he opened the door just a crack and watched as Butch crossed the street and headed for a car parked beneath the West Side Highway. It was a red Porsche with a New Jersey license plate – BYF 973. Michael repeated it to himself over and over until he was sure he had memorized it. He then waited until Butch drove away before emerging into daylight. It was raining again, but it didn't feel as cold as before. Burning with a new fever, Michael started walking at a brisk pace – and thinking. There was so much to do and so little time.

Fifty yards away, behind the wheel of his unmarked vehicle, Lt. Navarro lowered his binoculars and rubbed his eyes. What was once obscure was gradually coming into focus. Intrigued, he started his engine and pulled away from the curb.

XXII

Alice O'Hegan wasn't supposed to be working that evening. But when Mr. Pisani, the owner of Angelo's, called and explained that two of his waitresses were out sick, Alice couldn't resist the opportunity to come to her employer's aid. Not only were the tips good, but there were other fringe benefits. Although Mr. Pisani was a married man, Alice found him quite engaging. It wasn't that he was a particularly handsome man, just tall, dark and reasonably affluent – a vast improvement over the string of losers she had dated over the last twenty years. She would often entertain a fantasy in which Mr. Pisani left his spoiled, uncaring wife and, instead, swept Alice up in the middle of her shift and flew her to the Bahamas. Still single at thirty-seven, Alice clung to the hope that something more fulfilling than waiting tables and living from one paycheck to the other awaited her. After all, she was attractive, and even if she barely finished high school she considered herself well informed and street-smart. What's more, she had a keen memory. She never forgot a face and could recall a customer's order months after she delivered it.

"Don't tell me," said Alice. "A scotch on the rocks. Right?"

"Excuse me?" said Michael, snapping out of his reverie.

"The last time you were here, you ordered a scotch on the rocks."

"You remember, huh?"

"Mmm-hmm. You were here with Butch."

The name struck an anxious chord in Michael. "That's right," he replied. "So you know Butch?"

"Know him?" scoffed Alice. "He's been coming here for years."

"That's just his nickname, right?"

Alice regarded Michael with a quizzical expression. "Well, of course. Aren't you two friends?"

Michael practically bristled at the suggestion. "Acquaintances," he corrected. "I ... hired him for a job."

"Oh, really? How did it go?" Alice casually inquired, obviously unaware of Butch's true profession.

"Better than I had hoped," said Michael ironically. "The thing is," he added, "we've lost track of each other and I don't know how to reach him. I don't suppose you would know where I can contact him?"

"Gee, I wish I could help you," said Alice. "He comes here alot, but not on any particular night."

"Do you know where he lives?" asked Michael.

"No, I don't. Although ... he has mentioned owning a house in New Jersey."

"Did he say where in New Jersey?"

Alice thought hard. "Just over the river. On the Palisades. I know because he's always bragging about his view of Manhattan. What's the name of that place?" Alice racked her brain.

"Weehawken?" Michael offered.

"It wasn't Weehawken ..."

"Jersey City?"

"No ..."

"Union City?"

"No ..."

"Fort Lee?"

"No. It was one word. Oh, well," sighed Alice. "I can't remember. All I know is that it's right on the edge of the river."

"Edgewater," blurted Michael.

"That's it!" Alice exclaimed. "Edgewater. Whew! Now you can look him up in the phone book."

"I would if I knew his real name," Michael replied with a purposefully giddy laugh. The last thing he wanted to do was arouse suspicion. "I never caught his surname. I just know him as Butch."

Alice put her thinking cap back on. Butch often charged his meals. Her photographic memory zeroed in on the name on his credit card. "Mussante," she declared. "Michael Mussante."

Michael? Michael winced.

At that moment, a customer at another table caught Alice's eye. "Will you excuse me for a minute, hon? I'll be back to get your order."

"Take your time," smiled Michael, lifting his menu. "I haven't yet decided what I want."

****

Naturally, there was no listing for an M. or Michael Mussante in the Edgewater, Weehawken or Fort Lee telephone directories. Nor could Information produce a number or an address. All Michael had to go on was that Butch's house was located along the Palisades, just across the Hudson River from Manhattan. It was a longshot, but he decided to investigate. He called in sick the next day, rented a compact car and took a late morning ride to New Jersey via the Lincoln Tunnel.

Exiting in Weehawken, Michael drove to the easternmost boulevard overlooking the Hudson River and slowly headed north. To his right was a stunning view of Manhattan, to his left a row of upscale apartment buildings amid scatterings of two-family houses. A mile or so later, the road veered right down a winding hill toward the riverside. Along the route were docks with ferry boat services, a few modest shopping malls and several industrial facilities. Finally, several miles from where the search began, Michael noticed a sign indicating that he was entering Edgewater. Indeed, there were many private houses along the roadside, some set in the jagged cliffs facing the river. Few, however, had automobiles parked outside their garages or sheltered under modest carports, and none sported a shiny red Porsche.

Undaunted, Michael continued his search, pulling off the road on occasion to allow other impatient motorists to pass him. He was determined to take as much time as necessary to check each and every house. Much to his chagrin, the road eventually led Michael into another township. Edgewater, Alice had told him with certainty. Edgewater, New Jersey. Accordingly, he made a U-turn and headed back south. Perhaps he had missed the red Porsche. Or maybe Butch wasn't home during the day. Maybe Michael would get lucky and spot it elsewhere along the route. Hoping so, he drove back to the shopping mall and cruised the parking lot. Then it was back on what he now knew was River Road, passing the same houses again as he headed north. Determined, he repeated the cycle over and over again – north through Edgewater, south through Edgewater – until he was sure that no house facing the river had been overlooked.

And then it happened. Michael routinely stopped at a red light and reflected on his obsession, starting to question his sanity, all but accepting the futility of his quest. Suddenly, a blaring horn startled him from his reverie, a restless driver behind him calling his attention to the green light. As he impulsively took his foot off the brake and accelerated, Michael glanced in his rear view mirror, then did a quick double take. *The car following him was a red Porsche.*

Tightly gripping the steering wheel, Michael proceeded well below the speed limit. The male driver of the red Porsche, shrouded behind the tinted glass of his windshield, tailgated the rented car, occasionally veering left to check oncoming traffic, obviously annoyed but unable to pass. Gathering his wits, Michael switched on his hazard blinkers and veered toward the shoulder of the road. Seizing the opportunity, the red Porsche swung around him. Michael deliberately raised his left hand and massaged his temple, denying the driver a clear view of his face. As the sportscar roared by, Michael noted the Garden State license plate number - BYF 973.

With his heart pounding, Michael accelerated to follow the Porsche at a reasonable distance. Surely it was Butch behind the wheel, probably heading for home. Yes, it was *definitely* Butch because Michael had to maintain a pace ten miles above the speed limit around winding curves so as not to lose him. What was the rush? Did he suspect he was being followed? Or was Butch just flaunting the superior performance of his vehicle? Michael feared that he would leave him in the dust. But as they approached an intersection, Michael also feared that they would both be stuck at the changing traffic light, that all Butch would have to do was glance in his rearview mirror and recognize Michael's face. He held his breath as the light turned from yellow to red, waiting for Butch to slam his brakes.

Instead, Butch recklessly sailed through the red light, leaving Michael no alternative but to come to a screeching halt or risk a collision. "Shit!" he hissed, thumping his steering wheel and watching as the red Porsche disappeared around another bend in the road.

When the light finally changed, Michael proceed at normal speed, hoping against hope that he could pick up Butch's trail. He didn't have to drive far. As he approached a series of cliffside houses, he spotted the red Porsche parked in the driveway of a plain, white, aluminum-sided ranch. Michael paused along the shoulder of the road to note the address nailed in bold black numbers on the front door archway. Then, fearing discovery, he drove on, heading north toward the George Washington Bridge and a route back to the city.

Along the way, Michael struggled to contain his curious mixture of exhilaration and anxiety. For once he knew what it felt like to be both the hunter and the hunted. He considered and rejected a host of alternatives. No matter how he wrestled with his conscience, his will to survive was overpowering. Invariably, his soul-searching led to one – and only one – conclusion: It was time to thaw out the gun.

XXIII

It was undeniably cold that evening, colder than it had been in several weeks thanks to an arctic front rushing down from the northwest like a freight train. Even with the car's heater blowing full blast, Michael felt the numbing chill in his bones. He had resolved not to think about where he was going or why. He had a tendency of thinking too much, and when he did it had a way of changing his mind. The less he thought tonight, the better. This was a time to act, not to deliberate. There were no choices left, anyway, no convenient moral or intellectual escape clauses. He had been down this grim, lonely road before. Only this time, there would be no turning back.

Driven by a sense of urgent purpose, Michael found his way back to Butch's house, parking his rental car in the lot of a boat basin a few hundred feet down the road and along the river. He stood beside his vehicle for a moment, gaping in awe at the spectacular view of a bejeweled Manhattan, taking deep breaths and exhaling frosty fumes of fear and exasperation. *Just do it*, he prodded himself. *Don't think. Don't think.*

He consulted his wristwatch – 10:15 p.m. – and then began trudging on foot toward his uncertain destiny. The pearl-handled Beretta in his coat pocket, having been retrieved from the frigid recesses of his freezer, was still icy cold to the touch, but nevertheless unlocked and loaded.

When he reached his destination, Michael carefully crossed

the road and scrambled unseen up the sloping empty driveway. He peered through a window into the attached garage, but didn't see a trace of the red Porsche. *Good*, he thought. Butch was out for the evening. Michael was counting on the element of surprise. The idea of ringing Butch's doorbell and gaining access by pretending to be delivering money probably wouldn't have worked. Butch would have been suspicious, demanding to know how Michael had tracked him down. One moment's hesitation on Michael's part and Butch could easily disarm him – or worse.

Somehow, Michael had to get into the house and lay in wait for his intended victim. But how? He went to the front door, but there was no welcome mat, let alone a key underneath it or over the door frame. And even if there were, who knew if the house had a security system? So Michael wandered around the property like a common prowler, searching in vain for an unlocked window or any other easily accessible means of entry. Eventually, his inspection focused on the foundation of the house and he realized that it had a basement.

It was too dark to see anything inside, but crouching low Michael could tell that the narrow basement window was not wired to an alarm. Gingerly, he removed the Beretta from his pocket, engaged the safety, then used the handle to punch a hole in one of the panes. The shards of glass fell inward, making more noise than Michael had hoped. He paused and nervously scanned the surrounding yard, fearful until he felt assured that no one beyond the perimeters of the property had heard the sound. Then he slipped the Beretta back into his coat pocket, reached cautiously through the shattered pane and unhooked the window latch. Slithering feet first, he climbed through the open window, barely squeezing through, and plunged into a pitch black void, landing safely on what felt like a concrete floor.

Michael stood perfectly still for a moment, hoping his eyes would adjust to the darkness. He had foolishly neglected to bring a flashlight or matches and the only trace of faint illumination came from what might have been a surge protector or appliance in a corner of the room. He began to take small, tentative steps, reaching out like a blind man groping for any unseen obstacles.

Inching forward, his left foot abruptly struck something hard and metallic, almost tripping him. Michael veered to the right, his hands swaying in the air until one of them miraculously found a dangling cord. He tugged on it, switching on a naked light bulb that glared like a camera flash. Suddenly, a startling, looming figure he momentarily mistook for a hanged body came into view. Michael gasped, lost his balance and fell backward to the floor. Looking up, he confronted the apparition – a heavily-padded dummy suspended from a rafter. Its groin was emasculated, torn open and bleeding thick bales of white fiber.

"Christ," Michael muttered, feeling and actually *hearing* his heart throbbing wildly in his chest.

As it gradually settled down, he got to his feet and looked around the room. In one corner was a full-size refrigerator flanked on each converging wall with boxes and file cabinets. On the other side of the basement were a washer and a dryer and aluminum shelves stocked with tools and cleaning products. Behind a wooden staircase were a rusty old water heater and an oil burner that automatically clicked on in the chill of the draft from the broken window.

As innocuous as it was, the basement nevertheless gave Michael the creeps. God only knew what Butch kept in that refrigerator. And looking up at the low ceiling with its veins of copper pipes and serpentine electrical wires, Michael felt as if he were trapped in the bowels of a sleeping beast. Composing himself, he drifted toward the nearby staircase. Taking one creaking plank at a time, he slowly climbed the steps until he came to a foreboding red door. He paused, mustering his courage, then quietly turned the knob.

Crossing the threshold, Michael found himself in a darkened kitchen. Distant streetlights shining through a window cast eerie shadows on the wall, providing enough of a glow to accommodate his path. He pressed on, traipsing lightly over the linoleum flooring toward an archway leading to the dining room. There he paused again, listening curiously and detecting a soft pattering sound. The wind in the woodwork? And where was it coming from? He glanced back into the kitchen, along a row of cabinets, the sink and another refrigerator – and then down on the floor. It was there, beside a wastebasket, that he noticed two plastic feeding bowls.

A sudden growl made Michael flinch. He peered into the darkness of the dining room and eventually noticed a pair of red eyes staring back at him from under the table. Transfixed, he didn't dare move. Nevertheless, his mere presence provoked another deep, guttural growl, the kind only a guard dog would issue as prelude to an attack. Had Michael known the house was protected, he would never have trespassed. Why hadn't the dog barked when he broke the window to gain entry, he wondered. Surely, it must have heard him stumbling around in the basement. Why didn't it react? Unless …

Michael suddenly recalled the dummy with the tattered groin hanging from the rafters in the basement. *He trained him*, he realized, *trained him to ambush unsuspecting intruders.*

"Good dog," Michael uttered against his better judgment, a pacifying gesture that only succeeded in arousing greater hostility in the Doberman and the flash of her merciless fangs. "Ssshhh ..." Michael softly whispered, reaching ever so gently into his coat pocket.

With a sudden bolt, the beast sprang forward. Michael quickly whipped out the Beretta, aimed and pressed the trigger. But nothing happened – he had forgotten to release the safety. Before Michael could react, the Doberman pounced against his chest, sending him sprawling to the kitchen floor and knocking the gun away.

The beast lunged for his throat, but Michael defensively raised his padded arm, wedging it between the canine's jaws. As the dog tugged wildly on the sleeve of his coat, Michael groped in vain for his weapon. He was surprised at the weight of the animal, practically pinning him to the floor. Yet its viciousness got his adrenaline pumping.

With all the strength he could gather, he brought his other arm around and managed to grab hold of the canine's collar. With one powerful tug, he sent the dog tumbling across the floor and slamming against a leg of the kitchen table. It gave Michael a few seconds to roll over on his belly and search frantically for the Beretta. But just as he laid his hands on the gun, he felt a sharp, piercing pain in his left ankle. He cried out in anguish as the Doberman drew blood and he twisted his body around. In desperation, he kicked the dog in the head repeatedly with the heel of his right shoe. But the crazed animal would not relent, its jaws locked and its incisors gnawing mercilessly on Michael's helpless limb.

"Goddamn bitch!" he shouted, bending his knee and thrusting his foot against the dog's chest with all his might. The force of the blow was so powerful that it propelled the Doberman against the refrigerator and elicited a horrid yelp. Before the creature could shake off the impact and resume its attack, Michael clicked off the safety. As the dog sprang again, Michael clutched the Beretta with two hands and pulled the trigger.

The shot reverberated in Michael's ears for a full minute. When the ringing subsided, he propped himself up on his elbows and stared at the still, black mass on the floor. There was no question that the dog was dead, its blood splattered on the white refrigerator door. Michael let out a sigh. *Better him than me*, he thought without remorse.

Eventually, Michael tried to get up, but winced as he put weight on his left ankle.He touched the wound to get an idea of its severity. Fortunately, it wasn't as deep as he had feared, and there wasn't that much blood seeping into his socks. Clutching the edge of the kitchen table and gritting his teeth, Michael struggled to his feet and limped to the sink. He placed the Beretta on the countertop, opened the faucet and let the water run until it was warm. Then he removed a handkerchief from his pants pocket, soaked it and knelt down to tie the wet bandage tightly around his throbbing ankle.

When he rose, Michael felt light-headed, so he took several deep cleansing breaths, cupped his hands and doused his face with cold water. Then he shut the faucet, picked up the Beretta, and cradled it in his arms, letting the reality of the moment set in. Now he truly was beyond the point of no return. Yet, he was plagued with the usual doubts. It was one thing to kill a wild animal, but did he have the intestinal fortitude to kill a man? *Don't think!* But how could he not follow through on his premeditated plan? It wasn't only his skin he was protecting, he insisted. *Think of Cynthia. Hell, think of Alan. An eye for an eye. Fight fire with fire.* That's what it came down to – fighting fire with fire, survival and, perhaps, redemption.

There was no point in removing and hiding the animal's carcass. Butch wouldn't have time to discover it. He wouldn't have time for much of anything. Michael would do what he had to do as swiftly as possible, the moment Butch walked through the front door. One well-placed shot would do the trick – two or three if necessary. Like he had done at the shooting range when he was practicing for his showdown with Leon Wendt.

Don't think! Just aim and fire!

Keeping as much weight off his left foot as he could, Michael slowly limped through the archway and headed toward the living room. He just wanted to sit down somewhere, Beretta in hand, and wait.

But before he reached the nearest chair, Michael suddenly sustained a hard, precise blow to the back of his neck. Supernovas flashed before his eyes. His legs crumbled beneath him, and his body began free-falling in slow motion into what seemed like a dark, bottomless well. He hardly it when he hit the floor with a resounding thud. But before he completely lot consciousness, he did see and recognize one small detail – a fine pair of imported black boots.

XXIV

―――――――――――――

"Wake up," said a distant voice. Michael heard it clearly, but couldn't respond. He was too immersed in a fluid dream, floating underwater in a sea without a surface. There was no escape, yet no need for panic. The sea was still, silent, and as infinite and empty as space itself. He was safe there, invisible even to himself.

"Come on, wake up," the voice demanded louder. The noise was accompanied by several rather hard slaps to his face. The waterworld began to dissolve and Michael felt himself rising toward a bright light. He squinted and turned his head to one side to avoid the harsh glare of a ceiling fixture. Gradually, his surroundings came into focus.

He was slumped in an upholstered easy chair. Judging by other furniture, he was in a living room. But he wasn't alone. Standing tall, hovering over him, was Butch looking none too pleased with his uninvited guest.

"You killed my dog," Butch declared incredulously. "I don't fuckin' believe it. *You killed my dog.*"

"I ... I had no choice," Michael falteringly replied.

"What?" asked Butch, craning his head and cupping his ear.

"I ... I ..."

"Shut the fuck up!" Butch ordered, slapping Michael upside the head. "Don't you say another word, you spineless, worthless prick!" he angrily warned, spewing saliva. "What's the matter with you? Are you out of your mind? You break into my house – *my house* – and you put a bullet in my dog ... That dog cost me $2000. She had a fuckin' pedigree, for Christ's sake!"

Dazed as he was, Michael had the presence of mind to wonder what Butch had done with his Beretta. Fortunately, he wasn't holding it. He had never seen Butch like this before – so agitated, so surprised, so apprehensive. It was a revelation. It was almost as if he were human after all.

"But you didn't come here to kill my dog, did you?" Butch surmised with a crazed look in his eyes. "You came here to pay *me* a visit." He shook his head and smirked. "I don't know what's funnier – that you shot my dog or that you actually thought you could get the drop on me. *Me!*"

Michael didn't see the humor in either unpleasant task. All he could see was the stark reality of his present situation. He had failed in his mission and now he was at the mercy of a professional killer – and one who felt threatened at that.

"Well, I've got good news and I've got bad news," said Butch, leaning forward, getting in Michael's face. "The good news is that I'm not going to kill you. The bad news ... *is that I'm not going to kill you.*"

Suddenly, Butch grabbed Michael by the lapels of his coat, lifted him out of the chair, then cold-cocked him with a stinging right jab. Michael hit the floor, immediately tasting a trickle of blood in the corner of his mouth. "When I get through with you," Butch warned, "you're going to spend the rest of your life eating through a straw." To punctuate his statement, Butch rendered a swift kick to Michael's ribs. Michael grunted and rolled over on his side. "Then, I'm gonna' ransack your apartment and hock every piece of jewelry and valuable possession you own until I have the money you owe me," he added, kicking Michael again. "And *then,* I'm gonna' find your girlfriend, tie her up, rape her all night and put a bullet in her skull using your gun! How's that for payback, you lousy ..." Kick. "...gutless" Kick. "... piece of shit!"

Michael clutched his sides and groaned in agony.

"You should have paid me when you had the chance," Butch chastised, looming over him. "Then I would have gone away and you could have had your ..." Another hard kick. "... *MISERABLE* little life back."

Michael grimaced in pain and kept rolling across the floor in a useless attempt to escape. His eyes frantically wandered from one piece of furniture to the next – a couch, a coffee table, the chair he had been sitting in, a footstool a few feet from his head.

"You should have paid me, Mike," Butch lamented. "I mean, a deal's a deal. If only you had kept up your end of the bargain, your friend Alan would be alive today. Eh?" Then, in another flash of anger, Butch swung his leg and caught Michael in the abdomen, rolling him like an old carpet.

"AHHH!" Michael cried, sprawled on his back, clutching his stomach. As the pain subsided, he opened his eyes and saw a bookcase across the room. There, on the edge of the second highest shelf, stretching from hardcover editions of *The Rise And Fall Of The Third Reich* to *The Bourne Identity* to *The Silence of the Lambs*, rested his Beretta.

"But no ... you had to piss me off," carped Butch, hovering over Michael, bending down to taunt him. "You had to play this stupid cat and mouse game with me. Well, the game's over, pal, and you lose. Only now, you get to spend the rest of your pathetic life regretting what you did."

Without warning or hesitation, Michael reached out, grasped a leg of the footstool and swung his arm behind him with all his might, striking Butch squarely on one of his shins. The pain was so sudden and intense that Butch cried out and his leg buckled, dropping him to his knees. With another swing in the opposite direction, Michael struck Butch's head with the stool, leveling him with the force of the blow.

While Butch was writhing on the floor, Michael struggled to his feet and lunged for the gun on the shelf. Halfway to his target, he put pressure on his wounded ankle, felt a sharp pain shoot up the side of his body and took a spill. He glanced over his shoulder and saw Butch laboring to get up, blood trickling down his face from a gash on his forehead. Determined, Michael managed to crawl the rest of the way, reach up to grasp the first ledge of the bookcase and lift himself to his feet. As Butch rose from the floor and began to stagger forward, Michael wheeled around, holding the Beretta with both hands and taking deadly aim.

Butch paused and stared down the barrel of the gun, then at Michael, bemused. "Who the hell are you kidding?" he mocked. "We both know you don't have the balls to kill me. You couldn't even kill Leon Wendt and look what *he* did to you. No, you weren't even enough of a man to handle that, were you? Huh? Am I right?"

Butch paused to wipe a drop of blood from the corner of his eye. He noticed that Michael's hands were shaking and he couldn't help but laugh. "What do you know about being a man, anyway?" he taunted. "About taking charge and getting things done and putting things right? People like you ... all you know how to do is hire other people to do your dirty work. You're just a fucking *worm*," he scorned through clenched teeth, taking a step forward. "You're meat, Mikey. Nothing more."

"Stay where you are," Michael warned, unsteadily aiming the Beretta between Butch's eyes.

His nemesis sighed. "Why don't you just face it ..." he said out of the side of his mouth, taking another step closer. "You don't have it in you. You'd never forgive yourself."

Michael didn't bother to reply. There was no need for a witty retort, no reason to get the last word in. The truth was in his eyes and when Butch saw it, he abruptly paused, the cynical smile on his face replaced by a look of stunned realization.

Don't think, Michael told himself as he firmly pulled the trigger.

XXV

Close to the vest – that's how Lt. Navarro always played it when he had a strong hunch, but insufficient evidence. A week after he had followed Michael Gray to Pier 17, however, Navarro decided to put some of his cards on the table. He didn't want to arrange an appointment with Michael, preferring to catch him off guard. Yet he felt a surprise visit to his office or his home might put Michael on the defensive when he wanted him more relaxed and forthcoming. So instead, Navarro chose a relatively neutral site in broad daylight. He was aware that, in recent months, Michael had taken to running the path along the Central Park reservoir on Saturday mornings. It was there that Navarro would confront him.

It was a partly sunny morning, warmer than usual for this time of year, a refreshing change from the bleak, chilly weather of the last few weeks. Since it was his day off, Navarro dressed down, sporting a black warm up suit and sneakers as if he were out jogging. But when Michael trotted down the trail, he spotted Navarro lounging on a park bench with his arms stretched out and knew immediately that this was no chance meeting.

"Lieutenant," he acknowledged breathlessly, parting from the path, slowing to a halt with his hands on his hips. "What a pleasant surprise."

But there was nothing in Michael's eyes that suggested surprise

– or apprehension for that matter. In fact, he wore the perfect poker face, betraying only mild exhaustion. Navarro just smiled and nodded his head.

"Funny I should run into you," said Michael.

"Oh?" Navarro replied. "And why is that?"

"I've been thinking about you recently."

I'll bet you have, thought Navarro. "Well, that makes two of us," he remarked instead.

Michael glanced at the space beside Navarro on the bench. "Mind if I sit down?"

Navarro lowered his arms and Michael took a seat. Leaning forward, Michael folded his hands and continued, "I've been trying to come to terms with the whole ordeal we went through."

"We?" Navarro echoed.

Michael glanced at him, then stared at his hands. "I know you were as deeply affected by my wife's death as I was. Not to mention the trial and the verdict."

"Yeah, well, it wasn't exactly a walk in the park," Navarro muttered. "No pun intended," he hastened to add.

"I don't know what was worse," said Michael. "That Karen died or that Leon Wendt was acquitted."

Navarro scrutinized Michael's profile, wondering if he was being sincere. "I think the real tragedy is that your wife is not out running with you this morning," he sternly replied.

Michael turned his head to look at Navarro. His eyes were misty, wistful.

Moved, the lieutenant blinked.

"When you told me that Wendt was dead," said Michael, "I felt a strange sense of relief. All I wanted was closure."

"And now?" asked Navarro.

Michael took a deep breath and leaned back on the bench. "Now ... now I wish that none of this happened. None of it."

"Yeah," Navarro agreed with a sigh. "But it did. And quite frankly, Mr. Gray, I've been having a hard time getting my head around the idea that Leon Wendt committed suicide."

"Oh? And why is that?" Michael mimicked.

"It just wasn't consistent with his personality. I mean, this was a guy who lied, stole and murdered without remorse. He'd do anything to avoid taking responsibility for his actions. That's not the profile of a suicide."

"Maybe he gave up on himself," Michael suggested. "Maybe he finally realized that he had no future, no reason to live."

"You didn't know Leon Wendt," Navarro contradicted. "Not like I knew him. To you he was simply this despicable career criminal, a smug, smirking scumbag who sat in a courtroom all day and feigned innocence while a parade of witnesses testified as to his pitiful pathology. But I spent plenty of time with him, face-to-face, one-on-one. I interrogated him inside and out. I got a good whiff of the guy and I damn well know what made him tick. And I *know* he didn't kill himself."

"Then maybe you're right, Lieutenant," Michael conceded. "Maybe he was murdered and it was made to look like a suicide."

"Well, if that was the case," said Navarro, "then it was handled by a professional."

"Why do you say that?"

"Forensics couldn't come up with anything. Not one hair, not one fingerprint other than Wendt's. If it was murder, it was well planned and well executed, down to the smallest detail that anyone other than a professional would have missed."

Michael refrained from comment, gazing instead across the reservoir at the skyline.

"Coincidentally," Navarro continued, "a colleague of mine over in New Jersey's got an interesting case. It seems that some wiseguy suspected of being a hitman was found dead in his house. He and his guard dog were shot. Only, it doesn't look like your typical mob hit or a burglary gone bad. Someone apparently broke in, there was some kind of scuffle and ... badda bing! A bullet between the eyes. Nothing was stolen from the premises but, oddly enough, whoever shot him took the time to wipe the place clean of any prints."

None of this seemed to rattle Michael. He was as cool as a cucumber, entranced by the drifting tide of billowy clouds above soaring skyscrapers. Navarro marveled at his poise and all but envied his newfound serenity. "Do you own a gun, Mr. Gray?" he unexpectedly inquired, already knowing the answer.

"Not anymore," Michael replied.

"But you did."

"Yes. I bought it for protection after Karen's death. I had a valid license for it, of course."

"When did you get rid of the gun?"

"Recently."

"Why did you get rid of it?"

"Because it was dangerous, and also I realized that it gave me a false sense of security."

"How did you get rid of it?"

Michael stared at the still waters of the reservoir. "I took it apart and tossed the pieces into the river."

"Why would you do that? Why didn't you just sell it?"

"Because there are too many weapons in the world, lieutenant. I didn't want it to fall into the wrong hands."

"That's very commendable of you," Navarro remarked sarcastically. "Aren't you the least bit curious as to why I'm asking these questions?"

Michael shrugged. "I can guess why you're asking."

"Oh?"

"You have reason to suspect that the hitman found dead in New Jersey was responsible for the death of Leon Wendt. And if, indeed, Leon Wendt was the victim of a contract killer, the obvious question is who hired him?"

"I don't suppose you could shed light on that."

"I'm afraid not, Lieutenant. You see, Leon Wendt must have had a lot of enemies."

"That's true."

"But try proving it in a court of law."

"Try proving what?"

"That any one of them knew the hitman. You did say he was … dead, didn't you?"

Surely Michael knew that he was treading on dangerous ground, yet his bold indifference struck a familiar chord with Navarro. Years of dealing with the dregs of society, untold plea bargains and revolving door justice had virtually crushed his faith in the judicial system. Rather than playing his trump card, Navarro deferred to memory.

"About 10 years ago, my grandmother was murdered," he reluctantly revealed. "She lived alone in an apartment in East Harlem. She was robbed, beaten, strangled ... and set on fire." Navarro paused to clear his throat, then went on. "Nobody knows who did it. Some junkie, probably. But to this day, I can't understand why anyone would do such a thing to a 79-year old grandmother. God, I wanted to get my hands on the guy responsible," he declared, clenching his fists. "Fortunately, I didn't. Because if I had, I wouldn't have read him his rights. I wouldn't have given him the chance to cop a plea. I would have thrown everything away just to shove my service revolver down his throat and blow his brains out."

"That's understandable," Michael muttered.

"But wrong," Navarro firmly maintained.

"Still ... with the right lawyer, a sympathetic jury ... You know the drill."

"That's not the point."

"Then what *is* the point, lieutenant? "Michael demanded.

"The point, Mr. Gray, is that no one has the right to take the law into his own hands. We can't just appoint ourselves as judge, jury and executioner."

"Our conscience," Michael replied, "is the ultimate judge and jury."

"Unless you don't have a conscience," Navarro countered.

"Like Leon Wendt?"

The question lingered in the long silence that followed. Then Michael spoke.

"The way you felt about your grandmother ... that's how I felt about my wife. Neither of them deserved to die – and certainly not the way they did. Neither of them deserved to go unavenged. But it happened and life went on. Life always goes on. And if we can live with that, surely we can live with the loss of a Leon Wendt. Look at it this way, lieutenant – there's one less killer on the streets. Two, if you count the hitman. Is the world any worse?"

Navarro reflected on that thought for awhile as he watched the weekend joggers go dashing by. A cool breeze caressed his face. It was a rare moment of pure tranquillity – and clarity. He turned his head to look at Michael. His were not the eyes of a killer, merely the bleak windows of a soul scarred by disillusionment and loss. Whatever this man may or may not have done, he was hardly what one would call a menace to society. Besides, without physical evidence, no jury would convict him. Against his better judgment, Navarro decided to cut him some slack.

"What happened to your leg?" Navarro asked, motioning toward the bandage wrapped tightly around Michael's ankle.

"Sports injury," Michael replied.

"Must hurt when you run."

"I can deal with it."

"I'll bet you can," said Navarro knowingly.

"Well," said Michael, rising to his feet. "I guess I'll see you around."

"For your sake, Mr. Gray, I hope not," Navarro archly replied.

He watched as Michael rejoined the stream of runners and followed his gait until he vanished in the distance. Then, wondering what his wife and kids had planned for the day, Navarro made tracks for home. After all, it was his day off and the city would just have to survive without him until Monday.

XXVI

In his line of business Johnny Sabatino couldn't afford to jump to conclusions, but he couldn't sit on his hands, either. Things weren't always the way they appeared, but they usually were. People weren't always telling the truth, but they weren't necessarily lying, either. If something went wrong, somebody had to be held accountable, but it was important to know who was actually responsible. Trust your intuition, but check it out first – that was Johnny's motto. If you make an assumption and it turns out to be wrong, it could compound the problem. Then again, perception is everything. Keeping all this in mind, Sabatino put in a call to Carlo Torello and set up a meeting at Kennedy International Airport.

The location of the little get-together worried Torello – especially in view of recent events. But when he reached the service road where Sabatino's Cadillac was parked and saw that he was also alone, Carlo issued a sigh of relief, squeezed out of his own Mercury and greeted his boss with the usual bear hug. "Hey, Johnny," he said. "You're lookin' good."

The usually dapper don was dressed down in an ordinary white silk shirt, a pair of tapered black slacks, leather loafers and Ray-Ban sunglasses, so he assumed the compliment was a tribute to his fresh Bermuda tan. "Yeah, well, you don't look like you're doin' too bad yourself," Sabatino muttered, slapping Torello's protruding belly with the back of his hand.

"So what's with this airport shit?" asked Carlo in a jocular manner, nonetheless eager to get this over with as quickly as possible. He had errands to run, and wanted to get back to business as usual.

"I didn't want to talk at the club," Sabatino explained. "I got wind of a new task force probe and the walls may have ears. You know what I mean?"

Torello nodded.

"What can you tell me about our friend in Jersey?" asked Sabatino.

Torello anticipated the question, but was nevertheless uneasy. "I wish I knew, Johnny," he confessed. "It's a fuckin' mystery."

"Uh-huh. He owed you money, right?"

"Yeah, but not that much," Torello replied with a dismissive wave of his hand. "$15,000. That's all. Plus interest."

"He was late, though," Sabatino noted, looking to his left and watching as a jet airliner took off.

"Butch was always late," Torello claimed, trying not to sound too defensive. "Look, I hope you don't think I had anything to do with it, Johnny," he added with a nervous laugh. "I mean ... come on. I wouldn't make a move like that without permission. I'm sure you know that."

Sabatino faced him and smiled faintly. "Yeah, I know. I'm just tryin' to find out what the fuck happened. Okay? One of my guys gets whacked – in his own fuckin' house – and nobody knows why or by who."

"What makes you think he was whacked? The cops say somebody got in through a basement window. Maybe he surprised a burglar."

"What are you talking about?" Sabatino scoffed. "Nothing was stolen. Whoever did it shot his fuckin' dog first. Then him. It was obviously a hit. Only a professional could take out a professional."

"Maybe he crossed somebody from another crew," Carlo suggested. "I mean, why would any of our people be involved?"

"I don't know. That's what I'm tryin' to find out," said Sabatino testily. "It doesn't add up and I don't like loose ends. Somebody's responsible and I want to know who."

The two men took a breather while another airliner loudly took off. Then Torello spoke. "Just as long as you know that I had nothing to do with it. I mean, I'm runnin' a fuckin' operation. I can't collect from a dead man."

"Yeah, well, do me a favor," Sabatino instructed. "Keep your eyes and ears open. If you hear anything, anything at all, you report it directly to me. Do you understand?"

Torello nodded solemnly.

"Shit," Sabatino muttered, looking over Carlo's shoulder and spotting an approaching white car. "Airport security. Just follow my lead."

The car paused beside the two men and the uniformed driver lowered the window on the passenger side. "What seems to be the problem?" he asked.

"It's okay, officer," said Johnny. "I stopped short and he bumped me. We were just checking for damage."

"You can't stop here," said the security guard. "There's room to pull over about a thousand feet down the road. I can radio for the police if you need to file an accident report."

"That won't be necessary," Sabatino assured him. "Everything's okay, so we're finished here."

Then Johnny returned to his car and Carlo to his. Sabatino's Cadillac pulled away first, followed by the security vehicle. But Torello lingered for a moment, struggling to get the seat belt around his bulging waistline. Carlo was satisfied that Johnny still trusted him and that there was nothing to worry about. Too bad about Butch, but the disrespectful bastard had it coming. Too bad about the money he still owed him, too. But Torello would make good on it in a short time. All he had to do was skim a little less off the top for a few weeks. No big deal. And he had faith that Butch's killer would eventually be identified and dealt with accordingly.

What Torello didn't know was that Johnny Sabatino had a nephew on his sister side who needed a steady job and was eager to join the family business; that in a few months, after turning over every apparent stone and failing to uncover Butch's killer, Johnny would conveniently assume that Carlo had indeed arranged the hit. That, combined with the suspicion that Carlo was pocketing extra cash, would lead Johnny to clean house. Torello's body would never be found and Johnny's nephew would develop a talent for taking bets and collecting debts.

The seatbelt finally snapped into place. Snug as a bug, Torello started his engine and slowly drove off, thinking about all the cash he had to collect that day, but also wondering whether he had enough time to stop for a calzone.

XXVII

When she was a little girl, Cynthia imagined that she would one day marry a handsome prince and live happily ever after in his castle in the cloud. They would have 12 children – six boys and six girls – and ride horses all day and eat chocolate cake at every single meal.

When she was a teenager, Cynthia replaced her childhood fantasy with a more realistic game plan. She would one day marry a handsome movie star and live in a mansion high in the Hollywood hills. They would have only six children – all girls – and travel from one exotic film location to another and attend every award show under the sun. She would be the envy of her former classmates, eternally young and obscenely rich.

By the time she graduated college, however, Cynthia had adjusted her expectations to the point where he envisioned herself committed, if not legally married, to a reasonably handsome, reasonably successful man who loved her for who she was and would never dream of being unfaithful. Children were optional. A house in the country would be nice, but not mandatory. All that matter was being content, and at this particular moment in time, Cynthia was.

"Come back to bed," she implored, turning down the sheet on Michael's side of the four-poster.

Michael glanced her way. "I'll be there in a minute," he promised, modestly closing the bathroom door.

Basking in the warmth of afterglow, Cynthia rolled over on her side, hugged her pillow and gazed serenely out the bedroom window at the sprawling Manhattan skyline. She wondered if she would ever be happier or more in love. Life was good when one was in love, and it would only get better. Everyday frustrations were of no consequence. Time held no particular significance. Nothing really mattered but the way she felt that moment..

And now that she and Michael were living together in his apartment, it was time to rethink the game plan. From here they were surely headed for a deeper, more enduring relationship. Images of white picket fences and suburban lawns danced in her head, as did diapers and carpools and late nights by the fireside. They would grow old together, safe and sound in a world of their own creation. And if everything wasn't perfect, they would simply hold each other through all the storms and watch the clouds roll by. Yes – that's exactly how it would be ...

While Cynthia drifted off to sleep, Michael stood naked before the bathroom mirror and intensely studied his impassive face. He knew that if he stared at his reflection long enough, it would eventually become unrecognizable – which it did. Entranced, Michael gazed at the stranger that metamorphosed before him, and gradually opened the vault to his soul.

It was more than three months since the police had found the body of one Michael Mussante in his Edgewater, New Jersey home. No arrest had been made in the case and, in all likelihood, none ever would. As for Michael, his life was more or less back to normal. He was all caught up with his work, free to spend most of his evenings and weekends with Cynthia, doing the things that people do when they surrender to each other's company, playing it by ear, and rarely, if ever, dwelling on the past. Cynthia knew nothing about the whole Leon Wendt/Butch escapade, and he didn't intend to ever share the story with her or anyone else. It was, as they say, a secret he would take to his grave.

He had found the conviction to gather all his photographs and mementos of Karen and place them in a storage box, which he kept tucked way in the crawl space above his bedroom closet. He had offered her clothing and jewelry to her relatives, and what they didn't take was either donated to charity or sold. It surprised Michael how easy it ultimately was to let go of her memory, especially when he was intimately involved with another woman.

And yet, it wasn't as if Michael were in love with Cynthia. True, they lived together, splitting the rent and expenses. In her mind, this signified something. For him, it was merely a convenient arrangement – like having a roommate. Emotionally, she filled some of the void, eagerly providing for his basic desires in a relationship, stimulating him sexually and intellectually yet, sadly, nothing more. Nevertheless, that did not deter him from accepting her generous affection. Nor did he ever discourage the intensity of her amorous attention. Why should he? No, Michael would take what Cynthia had to offer for as long as she offered it and he would do so without guilt or regret. And he would go through life, with or without her, one day at a time, fulfilling his needs as a means of forestalling the great inevitable.

Such was the man Michael Gray had become the moment he had found the will to aim and pull a trigger – the man with deep, dark eyes who was staring back at him in the mirror. A man who had reluctantly discovered one cold night that, when push came to shove, he was capable of *anything.*

He could live with that.

About the Author

Robert Stricklin was born and raised in New York City. He began his writing career while attending Pace University, where he majored in English Literature and graduated in 1973. Since then, his articles, short stories, poems, critiques and commentaries have appeared in more than 100 publications including *TV Guide*, the *New York City Tribune, Newsday*, the *Palm Beach Post, Rolling Stone*, and *European Cigar Cult Journal*. He has also written marketing copy for numerous corporations including Jet Aviation, Bank of New York and American Express. In 1983, he was awarded First Prize in the Articles category of the *Writer's Digest* competition.

The father of two, he now lives in South Florida with his wife Martine and serves as an editor at LRP Publications, where he manages three biweekly, customer service-related newsletters.

LaVergne, TN USA
30 October 2009
162443LV00004B/2/A

9 780971 936287